# KENT

## By Thomas Horan

# Kent

Thomas Horan

Published by Thomas Horan, 2022.

KENT

**First edition. June 23, 2022.**

ISBN: 979-8201190477

Written by Thomas Horan.

# Also by Thomas Horan

Kent

Watch for more at https://sickslickproductions.com/.

Nobody writes a book alone, and this one is no exception. Thanks firstly to Draft2Digital for giving me a platform to get my work out there.

Second (but really the big first) goes to my family. My parents, siblings, and relatives have put up with me for years saying I'm going to write books, and they never made me feel like I was a fool for thinking it. Special thanks to my cousin Sarah Morse Adams for showing me the way to independent publishing.

Most of all, special thanks to my wonderful fiancé Sasha and my stepson Nelson, who taught me how to be a man and who gave me the courage to keep going.

# 1.

"**Y**ou want to talk about *what*?"

The old man gaped up at the college-age girl that had come to his table out of the blue and asked her night-ruining question. His root beer, which he had been raising to his lips to take a swig of, now hung in mid-air in his hand like a gavel about to be pounded. Sweat festered on the top of his balding head.

The girl's face didn't change. She was a tall, athletic girl with brown hair tied back in a ponytail, a streak of blue contrasting it all tucked behind her left ear. She had her hands stuffed into the pockets of her dark duster; a leather messenger bag was draped over her shoulder. Her pale blue eyes never left his, and even in his growing discomfort, he admired that.

"Kent," she said, matter of fact. "I want to talk about Kent."

"Kent who?" He asked dumbly, stalling. Knowing full well what she meant.

It was Bingo Night in the dining hall, and it was still going on, had about another hour or so to go. Most of the other old-timers were in the thick of it, while those who hadn't chosen to partake had either shuffled off to bed or were about to. He himself was ready to turn in. The missus had gone back to the room half an hour ago, and was, God willing, already asleep. He hoped so; her insomnia had been hell lately.

But now he was starting to wonder if he was going to get any sleep this night at all. Now here was this girl, barely old enough to drink, appearing out of nowhere like a ghost, interrupting what had been a pleasant evening up until now and asking him about-

1

"Not who," the girl said. "Where. I want to talk about Kent, Maine."

And there it was. Like a light switch being flicked on, memories came back to him. The five of them in that stuffy office. The sounds of the phones ringing off the hooks. The cries of the scared townspeople. The lights passing over Webster's face on their late-night drive.

The screams.

The state of the town when they finally got there.

The figures...

He squeezed his eyes shut, blocking the sights and sounds out until they were nothing more than a dull roar. Once he was certain that the volume was down low, he opened his eyes again.

"Whaddya wanna know about that for?" he asked wearily.

"You're Jim O'Sullivan, right?" She sat down in the opposite chair without waiting for an invitation. "You were one of the officers that worked the case."

"I am." His fingers twitched on the table. His other hand finally remembered that it was still holding the root beer and set it down.

"I want to know about what happened that night. About why the town disappeared like that."

"What for, for Christ's sakes?"

"Look, I'll pay you." She reached into her pocket and pulled out her wallet. "I've got two hundred dollars on me right now. If you want more, I can run across the street to the bank and pull out more."

*Jesus Christ, she's serious.* He shifted uncomfortably. After all these years of flying under the radar, he didn't know how to handle this kind of brazen curiosity over an affair that was long done with.

Around him, the sound of the bingo game was in full swing. The helpers were going around and refilling water or root beers for the patrons too wrapped up in winning the grand prize, which tonight was a new rice cooker. The game went on, blissfully unaware of the two people eying each other in the corner of the room, or of the horror story that had gone unspoken for too long that was now in danger of coming to life again.

"Put your money away," he said finally, and drank from his bottle. "I don't need money. I'm not a bar performer."

She blinked, and then put her money back in your wallet.

"I'll tell you the story. Free of charge. But...are you sure? It's not a pleasant story. My wife had nightmares for a month after I told her."

"I'm sure," she said. A little too quickly; he raised his eyebrow, and she corrected, "I'm sorry, I just...I've been trying to find any information I can, and there's not much to go off of."

"There's the official record, which you can find at city hall," the old man said. "There are records of the Kent Committee in the courtroom archives, if you can stand to stomach all that bullshit. And of course, you can find newspaper clippings in the library archives-"

"But they don't..." She waved her hands in a wild gesture. "They tell me only bullet points. They don't tell me what happened. What you all went through. Or why Kent disappeared the way it did. No record in an archive is going to tell me that. Not like you can."

The old man nodded. It was a good answer. This girl understood, he recognized that; you don't work as a cop for all the years he had without reading people. She understood that reading and experiencing were two very different acts. She had read, had apparently already searched the records, but now she wanted to experience what no account would ever give her: the truth.

"In that case, we'd better order another round." He raised his hand to signal the passing helper. "Might even need two or three before we're done. Talking's thirsty work, and I'm about to do a lot of it."

He ordered another root beer, and her a water. That was another good sign; she wanted to be stone cold sober for this telling. She might need a drink before this night was over, but at least for now she was going to hear it in her right mind.

He drummed his fingers on the table, trying to figure out where to begin. The beginning of the story was always important, as important as its ending. The teller needed to set the mood properly, with the right words to let the listener know exactly what they were in for. Any less than that, and this telling wouldn't work. And this might be the last chance he ever had to tell it right.

He thought about it, and then he began.

"Disasters lose their importance over time, you know," he began, and he was pleased to not hear any shake in his voice. "Take that Malaysian airline that went missing a while back. Big fuckin' deal back when it happened, but now it's just a talking point on one of those *Unsolved Mysteries* shows. But you think the families of the missing find any entertainment in their loved ones being gone? Likewise, you think the relatives of Kent, Maine – the ones that are left, anyway – you think they don't feel that loss every day? See, the rest of the world, they move on. For those that lived through it, it won't ever leave us. You understand?"

The girl nodded earnestly.

"Good. You better." He took a sip of his drink and sat back. "Here's what the world knows: during a cold, dark week in November of 1960, the town of Kent, Maine vanished off the face of the earth. Poof. Disappeared without a trace. Folks still to this day don't know why. And with it went the town's seven hundred and twenty-eight residents, all disappearing into thin air. In its place, in the spot where the town had stood since its incorporation? Nothing but a crater the size of two football fields.

"Think about that for a minute. Seven hundred and twenty-eight people. A hundred and forty-one men. Two hundred and three women. Three hundred and forty-four children. I've never been very good with numbers – I'll probably mix up dates and times a good amount, and I apologize for that – but on that count, I've never forgotten. Not once. I'll be on my deathbed, and I'll remember that exact tally, because the numbers aren't just numbers. They were *people*, for Chrissakes, same as you and me, with lives and families and dreams for the future. You get that?"

"Yes," she said.

"You'd better. I won't tell this story to anyone who doesn't understand. I won't."

"I understand," she repeated. "Believe me, I do."

He did believe her. Or at the very least, he wanted to.

"Then grab that water and let's get started. I'll try not to ramble too much, but you know how it is with us old folk; the only way to shut us up is to give us our Ambien. And don't worry about the nightmares you have afterwards. I think a few nightmares every now and again are healthy. Just look at me: turning eighty-seven, and still healthy as a horse. And I've had my fair share of nightmares."

She smiled at this, but he could see the fear in her eyes. That was alright. Anyone who wasn't scared was a loon, in his opinion. This girl had her wits about her, by God. That was alright. That was perfectly okay.

# 2

The thing about the beginning of a story is that it's a lot like the first drink of the night. After you get past that initial bitter taste, the rest of it goes smooth enough. To really begin to understand why Kent happened, first you need to know what the town was.

The town of Kent originally lay about twenty miles west of Bangor. It wasn't a town you just stumbled upon driving around aimlessly; Kent had one road in, and one road out, and so they relied on the Bangor police office for everything. I think they had a sheriff's office with just one deputy, that's how small we're talking. They were a textile mill town, and that was about their only notable contribution...well, that and their distillery, which produced wine so good they had to roll you out of the bars because you couldn't stand upright on your own. Only a few farms, but screw it, it's Maine, you turn a corner and some asshole's growing crops, we didn't need more. Plenty of woods, as you'd expect, tree lines as thick as fog. The school building, they had housed maybe half the kids in town if they were lucky, and the rest had to hike out to the city for their learning. On the other hand, their church could pack the whole town inside it, which tells you everything you need to know. It was another God-fearing town near the Canadian border, but hey, they never bothered anybody. They were good people.

As I said before, any problems they had, they called into the Bangor police station, and in November of 1960, they did just that. That was my third or fourth year on the force; old enough to know better, but still a way to go to prove myself as a great cop. Wasn't until the Effie MacDonald case I worked in '65 did I start to come into my own and be accepted by the legends, even allowed to grab some beers with them on a Saturday night. But that's a different story for another time.

There were five of us in the office the morning that first call came in...this would have been the tenth or the eleventh, one of those days. There was me, who was writing up a citation for a couple of teens who were going seventy down a residential road the night before. Don't ask me how I remember that 'cuz I couldn't tell ya. It's always funny to me, the things people remember right before a life-changing event. Like that guy who remembered eating his wife's tacos the night before 9/11. Only time in history a man was saved by the taco shits, so far as I can recall.

At the desk across from me sat my partner, Peter Webster, who was manning the phone line; these were the days before we had official dispatchers. Webster was the best partner I ever had, before or after that week. He had joined around the same time I had, but a year or two older, and he didn't care for any of the bravado that a lot of those guys had. You hear about it all the time, especially nowadays with all the Black Lives Matter stuff; cops who join up for the badge and the gun, the bluster and the bullshit and all that. Not Webby. For him, it was about doing the job right and doing the job well. He was open and friendly, but he was there to do the solid work, and I always appreciated that.

The other three guys were taking a break and re-telling some bar adventure one of them had the day before. There was Derek Stugley, a man with a gut like a boulder and a mouth louder than a Plymouth's cherry mufflers; any chance he had to be in the spotlight, he took. Then there was Henry LaRose, who we all called "Trigger," who had the brains of a goose but on the firing range, damned if he couldn't shoot the wings off a fly. Lastly there was Frank Mongeau, who was pushing past sixty by this time but whose mind was still sharp as a tack, even if he was stuck doing desk work on account of the arthritis that had riddled his body. There were other officers in the department, but it was us five who were the leads when the shit hit the fan that day.

Stugley was the one regaling us with the bar story when the first call came in. Webster was the one who answered it. Even now I can still hear his calm, light voice saying, "Bangor Police Department."

"And so I says to him, I says, that if he didn't want to spend the weekend in the drunk tank, he'd better keep his hands to himself," Stugley was saying to us. "This fucking guy, he was just not having it."

"So he went in the tank?" Trigger asked, genuinely curious. He was the perfect stool pigeon for Stugley; he ate those stories up like Aunt Tessie's pound cake. I don't know what he ever saw in the stories, he had been on the job longer than Stugley at that point. All I can say is that he was a simple fool, and maybe he saw those stories as something to look up to, for whatever reason.

"Fucking A-right, he did. You didn't see that Santa Claus looking motherfucker in holding? That's him. Took two of the bouncers to help subdue him once he decided talking wasn't doing no more."

At this point in the conversation, Webster, who was still on the phone, leaned against the window and looked up at the sky, frowning. I noticed but didn't mention it.

"That's not how I heard it," I said to Stugley. "Chad Morrison said the guy was brought in quiet as a mouse, never lifted a finger or said a word once the cops showed up."

"Chad Morrison couldn't find his asshole with a floodlight," said Stugley, glaring at me more for interrupting his story than for contradicting it. "I was there, and I'm telling you how it went."

"If I ask the chief about it, hope he'll tell the same story," Frank droned in his slow, laconic voice. He didn't weigh in on discussions often, but he had a good eye for bullshit. He and I got along fine.

"Ask away," Stugley retorted, not backing down. He even puffed his damn chest out like a frog. "Report went right to his desk, same as every other."

Webster put the phone back on its cradle.

"What was that about, Webby?" I asked.

"Woman out in Kent." There was a look of concern on his face. "Says she sees a light in the sky."

"I seen a light in the sky too," Stugley said. "It was big and yellow, and when I stared directly at it, I got funny spots in my vision for a while." He laughed, like it was the funniest fucking thing in the world.

"Not that kind of light." Webster picked the phone back up and dialed a number.

"Who you calling?" I asked.

"Orono station. See if they can send their 'copter to investigate."

Me and Frank glanced at each other. Orono had a smaller force, but they were the closest with a working helicopter; ours had thrown a propellor blade three or four weeks before and we hadn't gotten it fixed yet. This was 1960, remember, and the police had only just started getting these things to play with. As a result, we only really requested them in an emergency.

We couldn't imagine what kind of problem a pissant burb like Kent would warrant a 'copter search, but it was Webby calling it in, so if he felt it was needed, then we went along with it.

"Is it serious, Web?" I asked.

"Not sure. She sounded serious on the phone, but-" He stopped abruptly as the other line picked up. "Hey, Orono? This is Bangor...uh huh. Yeah. Listen, your helicopter working? Yeah? Alright. I need a favor...yeah, I need you to fly over Kent. Lady there is reporting seeing a green light in the sky."

At that point, it was dead silent in the office. Trigger was staring blankly at Webster as though he had just been given a math test he hadn't prepared for. Stugley was looking as though the whole thing was a bad joke. I couldn't tell what Frank was thinking just from his face, but looking back on it now, I'm almost certain there was apprehension there.

In most stories like this, the main characters know right away that things are about to get bad. Well, I'll tell ya, that wasn't what happened here. I don't think any of us had any idea what we were in store for; not Stugley and Trigger, maybe not Frank, and certainly not me. All I knew was that in that moment, our office suddenly felt very cold, the kind of cold that doesn't have an origin, but settles on your bones like a winter frost. Poetic, I know, but I don't know a better way to describe it. I didn't know why it felt that way, but I recognized it all the same.

"Yeah, that's what I said. A green light. It...no, *I* don't see anything, but...no, I get you don't see anything either, but listen, this woman in Kent, she's in a state over this, I mean she's edging on hysteria, so if you could just...look, if it's about the bill, I will personally foot the funding myself, will you just send the damn thing to check it out?"

I had never seen Webster get mad before that call – the man had the patience of a Buddhist monk, even Stugley didn't get to him – but you could hear the frustration in his voice as he talked to the poor idiot on the other end. As it turned out, I was going to get familiar with this Webster very quickly as the week progressed.

"Okay. Thank you. I...yeah, I know, it's probably nothing, but...yes. Thank you. Bye."

He hung up.

"The hell was that all about?" asked Trigger.

"Don't know," Webster said, sitting back. "They said they'd get back to me in an hour."

I wanted to ask more, but that look on his face troubled me worse than my curiosity, and so I zipped my mouth shut and went back to my work. Couldn't really focus anymore, though. None of us could; even Stugley had stopped telling that idiotic story of his. We were on standby, waiting for a call we barely knew anything about to a problem we didn't understand.

As it turned out, the phone rang ten minutes later.

From Kent.

# 3

The old man paused to take a sip from his root beer. The girl was sitting still, not touching her water, giving him her undivided attention. Hanging on every word.

"Trigger was the one who got that call," he said next. "It was some elderly farmer who had seen the phenomenon while taking his cattle out to pasture. We watched the flurry of emotions crossing the dumb son of a bitch's face in real time, from alarm to confusion to the beginnings of abject horror. Would've been funny if we weren't so tense.

"His call didn't even finish before two more came into mine and Stugley's phones, and the two of us were subjected to our own introductions to that nightmare. Those two calls turned into four, four became eight, so on and so forth.

"By half past eleven, the calls were coming in faster than we could process them. Word got back to the chief, who in those days was Danny Jennings, and he went and dragged all the off-duty officers to assist. Every one of them was full of piss and vinegar when they came in, but once they realized what we were dealing with, they shut up and jumped in.

"The calls all varied in tone and urgency, but they all conveyed the same message: that morning, over the roofs and fields of Kent, Maine, a green light appeared and did not go away. Not like a manmade light, like a search light or anything like that. Not like a second sun or anything either. It was like that, uh...that Aurora Whatchamacallit."

"Aurora Borealis," the girl corrected.

"Yeah. That. The Northern Lights. It was like that, floating in the sky over Kent, only instead of multi-colored lights soothing them, it was a deep green light terrifying the hell outta them."

"Jesus," she said softly.

The old man nodded. "Crazy, right? And how do you think we felt, listening to all those calls? You think we thought they were all crazy?"

"Maybe." She shrugged. "But that many people all reporting the same thing...that's hard to believe it would just be a crazy prank."

He smiled. "You have a better head about you than others your age would. You're right, it's too many people to write off. Some of us may have doubted a little bit, sure, that's natural. But we took it seriously from the start, and we kept on it until the end.

"If that first call had gone to Stugley or Trigger, or hell, even me, I don't think it would have changed the outcome any, but it would have made our handling of the case a hundred times worse, because it's doubtful we would have taken it seriously. But because the call went to Webster, and Web took it seriously enough to put the call in to Orono, that set the tone for the entire investigation."

He leaned in closer, and she followed suit obediently despite the strong smell of root beer on his breath.

"Let me be clear with you: we did everything right. There was no mismanagement on our part. We did our job perfectly. If this had been an ordinary case, that would have been commended, instead of it being thrown in our face by the Kent Committee. But it wasn't our fault. We couldn't have known how things would turn out.

"In fact, it wasn't until Orono called back when it sunk in for us that something was going terribly, terribly wrong."

# 4

We must have fielded a hundred, maybe a hundred and fifty calls by the time they got back to us. Frank got the call. I had just wrapped up a call with a young mother of two when I heard him say, "Orono on line three, Webby."

"Got it." Webster switched the line over. "Yeah, I'm here. What did you see?"

There was a pause in the office, first one we'd had in an hour. Then he frowned.

"The hell do you mean? It...we've gotten maybe a hundred from Kent in the last hour, are you telling me they were all making it up? How do...okay, then you know what's going on, so why...yeah, yeah, I got it. Fine. Just keep that 'copter ready for another pass...don't screw with me, just do it."

He slammed the phone on the cradle and ran his hand through his hair.

"What?" I asked.

"They saw nothing." He got up and went to the water cooler. "They flew around the perimeter of the town for forty minutes and didn't see a fucking thing."

"Bullshit," Stugley spat. "Don't they know how swamped we've been?"

"They've been getting them too. Phones ringing off the hook. One of their guys apparently passed out from the stress."

"So, what, they're saying it's a big hoax? The whole town's in on it?"

"That's a hell of a conspiracy," drawled Frank. "There's over seven hundred people in Kent, the odds all of 'em are in on it are a long one."

13

"Right. Even if you offered prizes, there's always gonna be that one asshole who screws the whole thing up. I haven't heard a single deviation, have any of you?"

None of us had.

"And also," I added, "if they were gonna make something up, they'd come up with something more outlandish than a freakin' light in the sky, y'know? Really play it up."

"I don't know what to tell you." Web sat back down in his chair. "They flew up and down the town perimeter and could not notice any abnormalities from the air. Their word, abnormalities. Said as matter-of-factly as asking the weather."

Well, naturally that didn't sit right with any of us. We were still getting dozens of phone calls, the sounds of the landlines having long been drilled into our brains so that even when we went home that night, we still heard the ringing in our ears. Something obviously was up, regardless of what Orono was saying.

Then Stugley said, "Fuck it. Let's just send one of us out there and see for ourselves. If it's there, it's there. If not, then at least we'll know."

That sounded right to us. We all nodded.

"Alright," said Frank, "so which one of us goes?"

In the end, we drew straws. Not that we didn't all want to go – I don't think there was a cowardly bone in any of us, not then – but the station couldn't afford to send all five of us with all the traffic we were getting. Trigger emerged the victor.

We loaded his squad car up with some provisions to pass along if they needed some. We also gave him one of the shotguns, just in case. Nobody had yet reported anything violent happening, but it was better to be safe than sorry, and if there was anyone whose aim I trusted, it was his.

"Get in, assess the situation, and get back here," Chief Jennings ordered, as Trigger hopped into the driver's seat. "If I see any Dunkin' Donuts wrappers on the floor of this car, I'm docking your pay."

Trigger nodded, and he drove off.

As I said before, there was one road that led in and out of Kent from Bangor. It was about twenty minutes to and twenty minutes back, for a grand total of forty minutes. We knew that, and we knew that the timeframe was exact. So if he came back before that time, it meant he didn't make it to town. If he came back after, it either meant he had stayed for a cup of coffee...or something really serious was going on.

While we waited, we resumed our work. The calls had slowed down some by this point – after a time, it becomes redundant noise and everyone has had their say – but there was still plenty of work to do, as we still had to log every call and write up a report about everything we had discovered that day. Which didn't amount to much, of course, compared to what we didn't know it didn't amount to a snowball in a blizzard. It was menial work, but it kept us busy while we waited for news.

When forty minutes passed without any sign of Trigger, we didn't panic right away. The forty minutes were a straight estimate to and from, you see, it wouldn't take into account his own personal investigation. It was entirely possible Trigger had been waylaid talking to the town's citizens, or maybe he had disregarded the chief's orders and stopped for coffee and a powdered. Wouldn't have been the first cop to do it, nor the first time.

When the hour had passed, we tried raising him on the radio. Just to get a sitrep. He never responded. Instead, what we got was a high-pitched whine, like uh...white noise, like that. Like he was hitting the button at the same time we were. We tried again, same deal. After the third or fourth time, we gave up.

When one hour became two, and two became three, well, that's when we started to worry. It wasn't Trigger's style to go radio silent on important stuff. We ended up playing lookout, one at a time, alternating out every half hour or so, waiting for him to get back in. Still, there was no word.

At one point, I looked at Webster, and he looked at me, and we were both thinking the same thing: that something had happened. There was nothing we could do about it, though. We just kept working.

About three and a half hours in was when the squad car finally came back up the road. By then most of the shift had gone home for the night, and only a skeleton crew remained. I was the one on watch when I saw those headlights coming in, and I damn near broke my ankle running to sound the alarm.

The car pulled up and parked in the lot. Out popped Trigger, looking like he just took a trip through Wonderland. He looked around, whirling like a top as Webster and Stugley and I came out to greet him.

"How..." he sputtered, and when he turned to me, all I saw was total bewilderment, which somehow scared me worse than his absence.

"What?" I asked.

"How did I get back here?" He looked from my face to Web's, and then to Stugley's. "It's a straight road, there's no way I could have gotten turned around, so how-"

He whirled around again, as if expecting to be somewhere else.

"Jesus Christ, Trig," Stugley groaned. "Only you could spend four hours getting lost on a straight road."

Trigger whipped back around to us, and the fear in his eyes was so intense that I physically took a step back.

"Four hours?" he asked. "What are you talking about?"

"Look." I showed him my pocket watch. Webster did the same. We all let him read our collective time, which at that point was close to six in the evening. Trigger stared at our times blankly, then looked back at the still-running car. We all glanced in and stared at the dash clock.

It read two thirty-six. About thirty minutes or so after he had left.

And that was how the first day ended: with the five of us staring stupidly at a clock that was still showing the time from almost four hours ago.

# 5

"**N**ow I know what you're thinking," the old man said when he saw the disbelief in the girl's eyes. "You're thinking I'm yanking your chain, that Trigger was screwing with us to cover his ass."

"The thought crossed my mind," she admitted. "At face value, it seems impossible."

"Yeah, we thought so, too. I mean how could it not be, right? He'd made a mistake, reset the clock, something like that; stupid, sure, but maybe he could have. It wasn't until Webster and I made our own trip out to the town that we finally accepted the truth that the single road that went into Kent no longer went into Kent. But I'm getting ahead of myself."

Over in the Bingo area, a disagreement had broken out between two of the old-timers. The staff were trying to calmly break it up without causing more of a scene. Over at their table, the old man and the girl paid it no mind. Bingo was the farthest thing in the world away from them right now.

"The point is, you're probably expecting me to be bullshitting you, right? But that's the thing: I don't have to. This story is enough on its own without any, uh...any...what's the word again, the one meaning adding too much bullshit to a story..."

The girl frowned, her forehead creasing. "Embellishment?"

"Yeah! That. This story doesn't need any of that. A real true story doesn't have to rely on any embellishment or stretching to spice it up. A real true story can stand on its own and still give the listeners the same feeling.

"It's the same with horror movies. I hate horror nowadays. All gore and loud music and butchers wearing masks. The real horror is the stuff you don't see or hear. The stuff your mind has to fill in for you."

They stared at each other for a moment.

"You probably think I'm doing it right now, don't ya?" he asked. "Adding flair for the sake of it."

She smiled, just a small one. "A little bit."

"That ain't what I'm doing, though. I'm just trying to make you understand."

"I understand-"

"You don't. Not yet, anyway. But you will."

The waitress returned with their second round of drinks. The girl thanked her, and the old man took another swig from his new bottle. The dispute at the Bingo tables was resolved, and the game had resumed. The girl placed her new glass next to the first one, which had still barely been touched.

"Alright," the old man said, placing his bottle down. "Still with me? Haven't bowed out yet?"

She smiled and shook her head.

"Good. I like that. Let's keep going then."

# 6

At the start of the second day, I decided to make a call of my own. There was a guy I knew out in Kent by the name of Ernest Lanslow. He was a journalist for the town's news rag, *The Kent Korner*. He covered town events, school plays, festivals, that sort of thing. He was a good guy, and he was sharp as a tack. If anyone was going to tell me what the hell was going on in Kent, it was him.

As soon as I was in the office the next morning, I got on the phone and dialed his number. I got lucky; he picked up on the second ring. It was one of the few lucky breaks I got the whole case.

"Jim, you son of a bitch, how are ya?" he greeted me with. He sounded perfectly jovial, same as he always did, but I could hear a shakiness in his voice.

"Doing better than you, by the sounds of it," I said. Around me the phones were already ringing, though a lighter volume already than the day before. Still, it was the sign that the new day had begun for our station.

There was a pause in the conversation, then a sigh.

"Things are, uh...well, they're a mess, but I suppose you already knew that."

"Most of what we've been getting equals up to a lot of white noise about lights in the sky. It would be a bigger help to get a more grounded perspective."

"I can try-"

"Hey, O'Sullivan!" Stugley had come in and was getting set up. "Get off the phone with your whore and help us out!"

"I'm literally talking to a reporter from Kent!" I snapped back. "Worry about your own damn calls, will ya?"

He glared at me with the eyes of a firestorm, but I didn't back down. Stugley drove me crazy, and I imagine he never warmed up to me either, but he didn't intimidate me as much as he maybe wanted to. After a moment, he just grunted and sat at his desk.

I went back to my phone. "You still there?"

"Yeah..." Ernest's voice sounded distracted; I had a feeling he had been staring out his window, looking up at that light. "Yeah, I'm here."

"Start from the beginning. What happened?"

So, he did. What I'm about to tell you is probably the only official documentation of those first couple of days of the Kent, Maine incident, and the only account given by a member of the press. I'm sure others tried during that long, exhausting week, but so far as I've gathered in the years since, no one else ever did. Like I said, I got lucky.

According to Ernest, one of the first people to witness the phenomenon was a cotton farmer named Joe MacDuggen or MacDougal; maybe even MacDonald, ha-ha. Apparently, he had been getting the jump on the day's work, and while he was driving his tractor across the field he looked up and saw what looked like a green moon forming in the middle of the sky. In his words, it looked like a big beach ball hanging there. He didn't notice it getting bigger until about twenty minutes later, and when he did, he almost shat himself. The light had grown ten feet, and it was spreading out, no longer like a ball but more like a giant square, as he watched, the corners began to spread and divide, like the heads of that fuckin' monster Hercules fought.

He got off his tractor and busted his hump to the sheriff's office, but by that point a good chunk of the town had noticed the green light that was quickly filling up the sky, and were either already phoning the neighboring police departments, or they were also storming the town officials' offices looking for answers, and of course *they* didn't know what was happening any more than the farmers and mill workers did.

That whole day for them was pure mayhem as people talked and yelled and made their phone calls that we had been on the other end of. One or two families had gotten in their cars and taken off down the one road to Bangor. I didn't recall any cars showing up aside from Trigger's yesterday, and that made me uneasy.

Around five that evening, while ol' Trig was spending four hours failing to get into Kent, the town held a meeting. The mayor, Charles Caldwell, headed the meeting, and every member of the council was there: Paul Hackermann, Horst Schneider, Michelle Feinberg, and uh, the new guy...I'm sorry, I can't remember his name.

They met at the church, and for two hours the townsfolk went back and forth over what was happening and what they were going to do about it, and *if* there was anything they could do about it. There were some fool theories thrown out, according to Ernest – Horst Schneider had thrown out the idea of getting the military's tanks in to shoot the damn light out of the sky – and there were cries to evacuate the town, which were half-hearted at best. Ernest thought that most of them didn't want to leave their homes, although he couldn't pin down exactly why. Nowhere else to go, maybe.

It was the new guy, I think, who spoke sense to everyone. He pointed out that the light wasn't zapping anyone or causing mutations or anything like that. It was sitting there in the sky, harmless as a dandelion. Likely whatever it was didn't do anything but look pretty. We should just wait it out, he said, and see what happens. He had every confidence the situation would resolve itself.

Well, it wasn't the greatest solution, but no one else had a better one, so in the end the citizens got nothing but massive headaches for their troubles. They all went home and went about making dinner and going to bed. Although I don't imagine there was much in the way of good sleep that night.

"And what about today? Any changes?" I asked.

"None so far, but it's still really tense. Hardly anyone out on the street, and those that are just keep staring up at the sky as if they're about to get struck by lightning. You can feel the fear in the air."

"Jesus."

"I don't know-" He paused so abruptly that I thought we had lost connection for a moment or two. I was about to hang up and try again when his voice came back.

"Oh God!"

"What?" I asked, suddenly alert.

"I'll call you back!" And this time the line really did disconnect.

I had maybe a minute to process what had happened when the station phones, which at that point had only been ringing steadily, suddenly exploded like a Greek chorus singing in harmony. All the officers groaned as they dove right back into the same routine as yesterday.

That day wasn't as bad – about ninety-one or ninety-two calls, still a lot but not by much – and it was once more just a wind tunnel for noise, but here's what it all amounted to. And again, keep in mind I have no pictures or video or even my own experience to back it up. I only have the words of the damned swimming in my head.

At the time my phone call with Ernest was going on, the light in the sky had gone from a light green to a violent purple, looking almost electric the way it waved and flowed in the sky. Electric turned out to be the apt phrase, because after a while there were these, like, pulses, shooting across the sky in rings, pulsing every three seconds. Like those supersonic waves you read about in science fiction novels. They flowed smoothly, with enough force to shake trees and telephone poles and send birds flying for cover. Lights flickered but stayed on, and car alarms went off and turned downtown Kent into a symphony of ruckus.

That will do it for sure. I mean, can you imagine? Picture it, you're walking down the street, maybe you're getting milk for your family, and suddenly up in the sky it's like they're doing fucking atom bomb tests above your head. You see that shit, you don't know if it's radioactive or if you're about to be wiped off the map or contract every kind of cancer imaginable. At that point you're going to be out of your mind. Next, you're probably expecting UFO's or something.

What do I think it was? I have no idea, nor have I given it much thought. Of all the things that happened that week, believe it or not, that day has haunted me the least. Not that it wasn't a bad day; just compared to what happened after, it was tame.

If I had to place a guess, though...I think it was whatever destroyed the town, putting out feelers. Seeing what kind of...I don't know, opposition I guess, was in town. I don't know why I think that. Just nothing else makes sense to me.

Again, Webster had called in to Orono, asking for their helicopter to observe the activity from the air. Again, we had to wait while we sifted through hysterical phone calls from terrified citizens. And again, we got the call back from Orono letting us know that they could see nothing from the air.

Well, Webby lost his shit about then, and who could blame him? We all had been worked hard with all the calls, and here was Orono saying all of it was horseshit, it was enough to make you go to the loony bin. We sat there for another twenty minutes trying to do our work while listening to Webster call that poor dumb son of a bitch very terrible word you'd never want your mother to hear, while also asking how a bunch of special needs people got jobs as cops. I couldn't hear the other end, but I like to think the bastard was shouting in his defense; cops always like to argue with each other. This went on and on while we worked until Web finally slammed the phone down.

"Unbelievable," he fumed.

"Still claiming they don't see nothing?" asked Frank, smoking a cigarette at his desk.

"I don't know how the fuck you can't see a giant pulsating light in the sky from a damn helicopter in broad daylight." Webster fumed, shaking his head. "It doesn't make sense. It's like those people are seeing something that the rest of us aren't allowed to see ourselves."

"Maybe they are."

The words were out of my mouth before I realized it, but once it was out, it was out. The two of them looked at me; so did Stugley and Trigger, who were nearby. For a moment the only sounds between the five of us were the ringing of phones and the hustling of our co-workers.

"What's that?" Frank finally asked.

"I was mulling it over last night while I was trying to sleep," I told them, drumming my fingers on my desk. That's always been a bad habit of mine. See, I'm doing it right now! "I thought about it again earlier when I was talking to Ernest Lanslow. If you consider they're seeing lights while we're getting clear skies, and that nothing can be observed from the air, add Trigger's alleged story about never arriving in Kent-"

"How would I lie about that?" demanded Trigger angrily. "Seriously, how would I even be able to do that?"

I went on. "Then either the entire town is suffering a mass hallucination that someone else masterminded...or something wants only them to experience this phenomenon."

"Come off it," said Stugley with that obnoxious snort of his. "What are you saying? That the town is in some kind of special bubble where all this fucked up shit is happening and no one else is allowed inside or outside?"

I shrugged. Like I knew all the answers; I was practically a kid, for Christ's sakes.

I caught Webster's eye and held it. He was looking apprehensive, almost scared.

I finally heard from Ernest around five that evening, after most of the commotion had died down for the day. Unfortunately, I didn't get the full rundown of events this time; like I said earlier, there was only one full account of Kent, and it was given that morning. No more official records came out of that town, just the panicked accounts of its citizens.

Ernest's voice was calm, yet scared. He told me he was packing up and leaving town heading straight for Bangor. Said he had discovered something important, something he didn't trust would be received through the phone. He was going to come straight here, shouldn't take him longer than an hour. Time was of the essence and all that.

And I almost told him. I really did. It wouldn't have made a damn bit of difference one way or another, he was always doomed, but had I warned him, it could have maybe bought him a couple of extra days. A couple of days may not seem like a lot, but when you've lived as long as I have, you learn to appreciate the extra time you have.

But I didn't know then what I know now. And I didn't warn him either. I wished him luck getting out of Kent, and that I would see him soon. Then I hung up.

I went out onto the stoop again and waited. The sun was low in the sky and the temperature had dropped to a biting cold number. The trees were almost bare by this point in the season, and the roads were lousy with wet leaves that caused cars to go slow. There were quite a few cars that evening, but none of them were Ernest's station wagon. The longer time went on, the less likely it was looking, but I still sat there, hoping against hope that the station wagon would show.

There was a thump next to me. It was Webster, holding two mugs of coffee. He offered me one, and I took it.

"Any sign?" he asked.

"Not yet."

"Let's hope your theory proves false."

"Yeah..." I took a sip. "Yeah, let's hope."

We sat there for the next two or three hours, sipping coffee, not speaking, just waiting to see what the news would be, while around us the night life of Bangor went on without a care in the world.

Ernest never showed.

I never heard from him again.

# 7

There was silence in their corner of the hall as he finished this leg of the story. Around them the hustle and bustle of the Bingo game continued, although some of the members, having given up on winning the cooker, had gone off to bed. One of the Bingo aides went to the jukebox and put a quarter in; Buddy Holly's "It Doesn't Matter Anymore" came on, and the hall was filled with his melodious tones.

The girl sat there, mouth closed, a horrified look in her eyes that the old man appreciated; it meant she both believed and saw it for what it was. He took another long swig from his root beer and set it down.

"In the years following the incident, I have often wondered about what it was that Ernest wanted to tell me," He said, his voice scratchy from all the talking. "That's the one thing you won't find in any of the official reports, because I never reported it to the chief. It was pure speculation."

"Jesus Christ," she said again. "And...do you think he found anything...anything that explains what happened?"

"Ernest was only a local journalist, but he was good at his job. He knew how to get to the bottom of things. So yeah, I believe he discovered something regarding the phenomenon, and had either been silenced by someone, or he made it to the edge of town and got...what do the kids call it these days? Where they snap out of existence?"

"...Thanos?"

"Yeah. He got Thanos."

The girl snorted, but at least had the good courtesy to hide it in her arm. He grinned, not understanding why she found this funny but not questioning it. Brevity in a scary story was necessary, especially for the next leg of this tale.

Calming down, she next asked, "So what did he find that he couldn't tell you on the phone?"

"Well, I'll never know for sure," he replied, sitting back again. "But given everything that happened...and keep in mind, this is between you and me. Pure speculation."

"Of course."

"I think he found out that someone on the town council was orchestrating all of it. Either that or helped it along."

Now her eyebrows shot up. "What makes you say that?"

"You understand, I have no evidence to support this. It's just that I keep coming back to that new guy, the one who calmed them all into staying put. Ernest explained to me how calm the guy had been, how *sure* he had been, and that has always bugged me, because if you're that cool under pressure then why not try and convince them to evacuate until they knew it was safe to return? Either he knew what leaving would do-"

"Or maybe he was trying to keep them all in the same place," she finished. "For whatever came and took them?"

The old man nodded. "A possibility. After it all ended – this was around May or June the following year – I tried looking into his records, back when I remembered his name."

"It hasn't come back to you?"

"His initials have, now that I've been thinking on it. It was like, uh...R.F. or something like that. Anyway, never found anything. Possible I just missed it. It's also possible there was nothing to find."

Her forehead creased, and he could see her eyes staring down, looking at the table but not really seeing it. She was trying to find it, he knew. Trying to find what the hidden link was. He admired her tenacity, but it was fruitless in the end; if the best detectives in the world couldn't figure it out, this girl sure wouldn't.

"Well, in the end, it doesn't matter," he said, rubbing the bald pate of his head. "No bodies were ever recovered from Kent, and thus no way to easily identify the victims. None of the council ever popped up anywhere else either. It's all nothing more than pointless speculation, trying to find reason for the unexplainable."

*But there were still those nights, weren't there? Those dark cold winter nights where the thought still comes into your head and makes you wonder. Even now, after all these years, that doubt still lingers...*

He shook his head. "Anyway, I'm rambling. You don't want to hear the baseless speculation of an old man's thoughts. You want to hear about what happened in a small town on a dark week in 1960."

She gave him a supportive smile. "I don't mind listening. It's cool to hear your thoughts on everything."

"I know better, but I thank you anyway," he said, tipping her a wink. "So far, all we've had is bright lights in the sky and roads that no longer led where they were supposed to, and that's it. Things were bad, but not yet dire. The people were scared, but mostly keeping it together. We hoped that things would hold together long enough for us to figure out a way to get relief to them.

"Unfortunately, it was that third day when all hell started to break loose."

# 8

I had gone into work early, still hoping to hear from Ernest. I had barely slept the night before, tossing and turning and trying to figure out what the hell was going on in Kent. So naturally, I fell asleep almost the minute my ass hit the seat cushion. This was around five in the morning.

About two hours later, my sleep was interrupted by a barrage of ringing telephones and harried voices. I don't remember exactly when it had started up, but even in a half-awake state, looking around at my co-workers talking and scurrying at an erratic pace, I could tell this had been going on for a while, and I had somehow slept through the start of it.

"Nice of you to join us, ya lousy mick!" cried Stugley, who was putting on a hell of a show by having three phones on his desk at the same time. He had one receiver to his ear and his hand over the mouthpiece so he could snap at me.

"Whuh's happenin'?" I asked, sitting up and rubbing my eyes. Trigger placed a Dunkin's cup on my desk. Through my bleariness, I saw the panic in his eyes.

"It's Kent," he said. "Something's wrong with the kids."

"The kids? What?"

"Just help us out. You'll find out soon enough."

I got fully awake quickly as I switched on my phone and was immediately met with the harsh sound of the ringing. I picked it up and entered the nightmare of my own choice.

Sometimes in the early morning, the sky above Kent sent out another pulsation that shook the houses and awoke the already

31

traumatized civilians. An hour or so later, a woman named Sharon Meeks was alerted to the sounds of thumping from downstairs. When she and her husband went to check, they found their daughter Lesley banging her head against their living room window. She had been hitting her forehead against it for so long, she had left a blood smear against the glass.

When they tried to pry her away, her glazed-over expression suddenly turned, in Sharon's words, rabid. She started fighting and thrashing against them, headbutting her father in the face, almost breaking his nose. It may sound exaggerated, but Trigger insisted it to be the truth, this girl turned *feral*. It took both of them to finally restrain her, and afterwards all they could do was watch as she writhed and thrashed against the bedsheets that held her down.

Now, if it had just been that one child, that would have been one thing. But soon, just about every parent in Kent was calling into our station, all in a panic over their kids behaving in much the same way as Lesley Meeks. Kids snarling like rabid dogs. Kids fighting their parents like it was the Heavyweight Championship. One parent called saying that his son had bit him, had taken a chunk clean out of his right arm. Kids tied to their beds or locked in closets to keep them from being dangers, not just to others, but to themselves as well.

Why were they like this, you ask? We didn't know for sure then, and I imagine we'll never know for certain ever, but according to the parents, the recurring theme was that the kids wanted to go into the cornfield on the edge of town. Why? None of them would say, save one: a girl named Faith Chandler allegedly told her grandmother that she wanted to go "where they were." She didn't specify any further than that.

All of them begged us for assistance, for relief. But what could we do? Nothing was ever reported from the neighboring towns. Helicopters couldn't see anything from the air. The one guy we'd sent ended up right back here, having lost four hours without even realizing he'd lost four hours. It's not like we weren't trying, y'know, but we couldn't break through whatever barrier was keeping us out.

So for us, being unable to help them was bad enough. For Webster, though, it was like he was covered in a rash that itched no matter how hard he scratched at it. I didn't know what his stake in it was – not yet, anyway – but this had quickly become personal to him.

Around three that afternoon, he went into Chief Jennings' office to demand we send a detail into Kent to provide support and assist with evacuation of the town. The situation, he said, had become too dire to stay there. It was time to get them out.

"No one is going into Kent," the chief said. "Everyone just hang tight."

"They're going crazy out there! They need our help!"

"We tried to send one guy and he just ended up right back here without making contact. Who's to say the same thing wouldn't happen again? There would be no point."

"So we're just going to do nothing."

"We're going to stand by and continue to monitor the situation. That's all we *can* do."

Well, Web didn't like that one bit, but he recognized that arguing further was pointless. He stormed out, slamming the chief's door behind him. He went down the hall, maybe to the bathroom or the lounge, and we didn't see him again until towards the end of the day.

In our defense – and this might not sound like much of anything, but I feel it needs to be said – we all wanted to go. There wasn't a coward among us, every one of us wanted to get in a squad car and spearhead a rescue effort into Kent, but we were also realists. Trigger was the only one who had tried, but even those who still thought he was full of shit had placed that trip as the standard for any attempts to go to Kent. So, it felt pointless to try.

But that wasn't Webster's style. It was one of the reasons I admired him.

Nothing else happened that day, other than answering calls and promising help that would never come.

# 9

"I am curious about one thing, miss," the old man said as the waitress brought the next round of drinks over.

"What's that?" the girl asked, now looking a little startled. And possibly weary, if his intuition was still what it was, which he believed it was.

They had been at it for an hour. A lot of the players, having long realized that their chances at the rice cooker were non-existent by that point, had dropped out and gone to bed. Only the chosen few, the ones whose hearts and minds were really into the game and determined to come out on top, were still in, and even at their old ages, they showed no signs of giving up.

The old man leaned forward, staring at her suddenly earnest, and the girl shifted a little uncomfortably. The smell of root beer was now so strong on his breath that it overwhelmed her.

"What made you seek me out in the first place?" he asked.

She suddenly looked startled. "What?"

"I mean why did you come look for me? There are not many people around that still remember Kent, let alone that I was ever a part of the case. None of us were ever interviewed about it, none of us ever made a Sullivan appearance. The world forgot about Kent as soon as they heard about it."

"I'm sorry, I didn't mean-"

"Oh, I never complained about it. I never did the job for the notoriety, and after it was over, I just wanted to move on with my life. Not forget it, you understand. Never forget it. But not have it hang over my head like a fucking cloud."

She laughed, and that lightened the tense mood that had grown in the last thirty seconds of the conversation. She had a nice-sounding laugh, and one that, he imagined just from their brief acquaintanceship, that she didn't use often.

"So, what sent you my way?" He sat back again. "You look like you're college age at the earliest. Probably seen more of the inside of a library than the outside of a crime scene. I'm guessing you read some of the archived accounts?"

"Well, yeah, that was part of it." Her smile faded again. "But...well..."

"Go on."

"My great-uncle...my grandmother's brother...he was in Kent when-"

"Ah." He nodded sympathetically. "That would certainly do it. I'm sorry for your loss."

"It was rougher for my grandmother. I never met him, neither did my mom, but him and my grandmother, they...they were close." She swallowed. "Listening to Grams talk about him was like...like a window into her world, about a time and a life before me and Mom. I guess it just always made me curious. Grams passed away last spring. Emphysema."

"I'm very sorry to hear that." And he meant it, she knew. She could see it in the wrinkles of his face and hear it in his voice. "What was his name, your great-uncle?"

"Charlie Lewis. And my grandmother was Cheryl Lewis."

Again, he nodded. The pause that came was brief, but comfortable. It was like a bridge had been lowered that connected one end of a canyon to another, so that the two could finally have shared ground.

"She met you, you know," the girl continued. "At the memorial service they held that winter. She said she spoke to you."

"Ah..." He winced and gave a bitter smile. "I'm sorry, but I don't remember her. Please don't take it personally. I met a lot of grieving families that day, and they tend to blend together over time."

She nodded. It had been a long shot, but she felt she had to say it.

"So, you came here wanting to understand what happened."

"As much as I could, yeah."

"Well, I'm certainly happy to try. But I'll tell you right now, if you're looking for answers as to why Kent happened, I don't have them for you. There are some things that not even the smartest men in the world can figure out, and I've never claimed to be one of them."

He saw a brief flash of disappointment cross her features, but it left as quickly as it came. Maybe part of her had held that hope, the hope of finding the answer to her great-uncle's disappearance, but the logical part of her – and he had every reason to believe she was a logical girl – had kept her expectations in check. That was also good. It meant that now she could just be here for the story and not just the ending.

"Still want to hear the rest?" he asked.

She nodded. "Absolutely."

"Good. Because here is where things went from bad to worse."

# 10

In some ways, the nightmare ended on that fourth day. In some ways, the nightmare began on that day. Of all the days that made up that dark, terrible week, the fourth day was the one that has haunted me the most. Even to this day, when my phone rings out of the blue, I still think it's going to be Webby's voice, telling me that the worst had happened.

Ironically, it was the one day I wasn't supposed to be on call. Jennings wanted some of us to get some rest after three days of straight chaos so as to not burn us out, so Frank and I volunteered to take the first day off. Stugley needed the overtime for something, Trigger said he still had energy to go, and Webster, well...you couldn't pry him away from his desk with the jaws of life.

I got back to my apartment around midnight, dead on my feet and not in the least bit hungry despite my last meal being almost twelve hours before. I was living alone; I wouldn't meet my wife for another four years, and I never cared to have roommates. I collapsed onto my bed and immediately passed out. I don't think I even took my coat or boots off, that's how tired I was.

When I woke up, it was around ten in the morning, and I swear to you, I don't think I ever slept better before or since. Probably for the best, I didn't sleep well again for a long time after that.

My phone was going off in the living room when I came to. I missed it before I could reach it – I didn't have a phone next to my bed then, I was still too green for that trick – but I caught it when it started ringing again barely a minute later.

"Where have you been? I've been tryina' reach you for an hour!" Webster's normally soft, easy-going voice screamed into my ear, harsh and in a sort of frenzy. I was rapidly missing his old tone. I remember thinking I hoped this case ended soon, because I didn't much care for the person he was turning into.

"Aw hell, Web," I said with a yawn. "It's my day off, remember? Chief told us to recharge our batteries."

"It's been cancelled. We need you back here now."

"Christ. What's happened now?"

"They're gone."

"What? Who's gone?"

"Who do you think? They're all gone! Hurry up and get down here!" And he hung up before I could ask further.

But I knew. Even before I put the phone down and grabbed my keys, I knew. The entire drive down was clenched-knuckled as I prayed to God that I was wrong, that it wasn't what I thought, that I was still dreaming, and I would soon wake up...but of course I was wishfully thinking. One thing I learned repeatedly while working this case was that it wasn't bad enough that it couldn't get worse.

On that note, I was unfortunately right. When I arrived at the station, there was an even heightened sense of chaos, and a red-faced officer telling me that the worst had happened: that sometime over the course of the night, every single child in Kent, Maine had disappeared.

No one knew when it happened; according to one semi-coherent man, the kid had been asleep when he'd gone to bed, and then was gone when he had woken up. Not one parent could narrow down a specific time, either. The kids were there one hour, and were gone the next.

Can you imagine it? Can you just imagine it? Three hundred and forty-four children, almost half the town, gone at the snap of your fingers. Only thing I ever heard close to that was that fucking Roanoke Island where the whole damn colony disappeared, and no one knows why. It was baffling, and it only got worse as the day wore on.

That day we fielded a record of two hundred and twenty-one calls, a record that I think still stands today...not that it's a record to be proud of. Those calls were among the worst calls we ever received. Underneath all the fear and panic and confusion, there was that level of anger and resentment at us. That question of "Why weren't you there? Why didn't you help us?" That we would get from distraught mothers begging for any kind of assistance from us.

Let me tell you something: don't let anyone tell you that cops have no soul, no empathy. When you've gotten two hundred phone calls in a row of crying women screaming for their lost children and asking why you weren't there to save them...I don't care how tough you think you are, that would break anyone's heart. More than once I saw an officer have to walk away for his own mental health; Trigger was one of them, and he almost tripped over his damn chair trying to get away. Even Stugley got misty-eyed, the only time I ever saw the bastard show any kind of empathy.

And me? My gut felt like it was getting socked by the boxing glove of the heavyweight champion over and over with each call, and I had to suppress the urge to vomit a couple of times, but I didn't shed any tears. That would come later. Much, much later. But it hurt all the same.

Again, the request was made to send a detail out, and again, the request was denied by the chief due to the unknown factors. We were tearing our hairs out, I mean we were up against a wall here. All this shit and all we could do was poo-poo on the phone and act like polite operators to these hysterical people trapped in this nightmare for no good reason that we could see. We were helpless to see and helpless to help. In a way, we were as trapped as the people in Kent.

Webster and I went out for drinks at around eight that evening. Jennings ordered us, talking more to Webster that he needed the break, and on that note, I agreed with him. My partner looked as though he had aged ten years in the last week.

We went to Dell's, which was a tavern that cops and firefighters used to frequent. It's gone now – a clothing store now stands in its place – but that night there was a steady flow of patrons coming in and out, getting drinks, shooting darts and laughing away, blissfully unaware that thirty miles away, the people of Kent were fighting for their lives.

He and I got our table in the corner and a pitcher of beer for the two of us to share. We sat there just drinking, not talking, not eyeing the cute waitresses in their short skirts like we tended to do (What? We were unmarried men, it wasn't a crime), we just drank and tried not to think about anything; easier said than done.

I kept glancing over at Webster nervously. He had this look in his eyes that I didn't like. The year before, we'd had an officer named Tommy Donovan commit suicide; he had eaten the gun, classic cop suicide. While we all claimed at the time we never saw it coming, there had been a look in his eyes in the weeks leading up that we all should have recognized: a sunken, glazed-over expression that seemed to stare into beyond. That look was on Webster's face as we drank. The thought that he was having a mental breakdown had more than crossed my mind at this point.

After about an hour drinking and sitting in stony silence, he finally spoke, and his voice was all scratched up.

"Hey Jim?"

"Yeah Pete?"

He looked at me with bloodshot eyes, and it made me take another sip.

"Let's head out to Kent. Tonight. Just the two of us. Whaddya say?"

Well, that took me so by surprise that I choked on my beer. He didn't even flinch.

"You serious?" I asked, trying to wipe up the mess with a napkin.

"Dead serious. Never been more serious in my life."

"But Trigger-"

"That was three days ago. Things might have changed."

"Yeah, but-"

"Look!" He slammed his fist down and knocked his own drink over. "We're basing this entire investigation off what? One trip taken by an officer who doesn't have enough common sense to tie his own work tie? If you were the police commissioner, and I came to you and told you we were basing everything off of the wayward car ride of one officer with no corroborating evidence, what would you say to me?"

"I-" I clucked my tongue; I distinctly remember doing that. "I would want more evidence."

"Right. A second test. They do the same thing in science experiments."

"I was never much of a scientist."

"Jim, these people need our help. Who's to say tomorrow won't be even worse? At the very least we have to *try*, what good is sitting around on our dicks doing?"

"None at all."

"Exactly. So, what do you say? We go take a trip tonight. Right now."

Honestly, it didn't take much convincing. I wanted to help as much as he did, and really, what could it hurt? Trigger had made the same trip, and aside from losing a few hours of time, he was no worse for wear than he had ever been. Any way I looked at it, I couldn't see a downside to his idea. My only real concern – and it was a fleeting concern, I'm ashamed to admit – was those people who had tried to leave town and had just disappeared.

"Two things first," I said.

"Name them."

"First, we sober up. I doubt even the people in Kent want to be saved by a couple of drunks in a Ford Fairlane."

"Alright. Good."

"And two..." I paused, with my fingers pointed in the air, then said, "I don't really have a two, I just know we shouldn't be driving drunk in a Ford Fairlane."

We looked at each other, and then we burst out laughing. I remember that vividly. It was the only time that whole week we laughed, and we didn't laugh like that again for a good long while. We laughed and we laughed and I'm sure to the people around us we looked like a couple of drunken loons, but we didn't care. We were young, we had our whole lives ahead of us, and we were privy to a conspiracy that none of these people had a clue about.

So yes, we laughed. Like I said, it was a long time before I felt like laughing that hard again.

We sobered up and loaded his Ford with supplies for the trip. Mostly boxes of convenience store food we planned to give out to the first families we saw, as well as some medical supplies that we "liberated" from our medical office for the occasion (they wouldn't miss it). We had very little medical expertise between the two of us, but figured maybe the doctor in town could make use of them.

Web also brought his Remington. I raised an eyebrow when he placed it in the trunk next to the bag full of chocolate bars and beef jerky.

"You planning on going boar hunting?" I asked.

He shrugged. "Dunno. I get the feeling I'm going to be hunting *something* up there."

It was the way he said it that made me shudder. It was the lack of feeling in his voice that made me wonder what we were getting ourselves into.

We looked at each other hard.

"You ready?" he asked me.

"I guess I am," I answered.

We got in the car, started her up, and began our trip to Kent.

I'm not sure what you would expect me to tell you about our trip to Kent. If this was a horror movie, I'd bet you'd expect we'd see things: blood, scary images, and possible scenes from our lives, ghosts from our pasts. Maybe even see visions of our deaths, or premonitions of what was to happen in Kent.

I could tell you all of that. But I promised, didn't I? No embellishment. No bullshit.

So no, I won't tell you any of that, because none of that happened. We didn't see anything at all. The entire trip was remarkably uneventful.

It was the conversation we had on the way there that has always stuck with me.

# 11

The road to Kent is all forest once you leave the Bangor city limits. Nothing but thick trees for twenty some-odd miles. At one point the trees form a tunnel around the road for about three or four miles, and on sunsets during the winter, when the branches are covered in snow and the sunlight hits off the ice, it's the most beautiful sight around. Like passing through the gateway to Santa's wonderland. There were some houses along the road, but they were all abandoned due to foreclosure. They're still there; at least, they were still there last time I drove that way, about two years ago.

Once we were out of Bangor, it was dark and quiet. The only lights came from the dashboard and the headlights leading our way, and occasionally we passed a streetlight that provided a little help. We didn't turn the radio on; neither of us were in much of a music mood.

Webster was the one driving, and he was gripping that steering wheel like it was a life preserver. I kept glancing over at him, still convinced he was in the middle of a nervous breakdown. We drove in silence for what felt like ages, even though it couldn't have been more than a few minutes.

Finally, I asked the question that had been dancing around in my head for the last day or so.

"Is this...personal for you, Webby?" I asked.

He didn't answer at first. I wasn't sure if he was going to. Then he said, "Get me a cigarette from the glove box."

I pulled the pack from the compartment and gave him a smoke. Even lit it for him. He just smoked in silence for a long while, not saying anything. I was afraid he was just going to keep quiet. Then he spoke again.

"You ever hear of a town called Ichabod, Montana?" he asked me.

I shook my head. "Never been there."

"No one has. Not anymore." He rolled down his window and pitched the half-spent cigarette out the window. "It's a ghost town now."

"Why?"

"No one knows. Some say a fire forced them out, some say a disease ravaged the town. Still others don't think anything like that; according to them, the townspeople were there one day, and they were gone the next. Whatever the reason, the town was abandoned, the roads were reworked to go around instead of through, and the town fell into legend."

"That's all well and good, but what-"

"My parents fought a lot when I was a kid," he continued, and I stopped immediately when he said that. I don't think he had ever talked about his family before, not that I can remember anyway. "Dad drank a lot, but he wasn't mean; just sad. He was a writer with many books and no one who wanted to read them. Mom was an architect and excavator, and she was...well, she loved me, but she was angry. Angry at Dad for not making any money, angry at him for spending what money we did have on booze, just...just angry all the time."

I said nothing. I had worked with Webster for a while, and he wasn't exactly a secretive guy, but he didn't talk about his family to us until now. Until then I thought they were retired and living down on the Cape without a care in the world or something.

"I remember waking up one night to them yelling...well, her yelling and him barely being coherent. She told him she was tired of it, tired of him, and that she was taking the Ichabod job in the hopes that she could finally have money enough to take me and leave. I drifted back to sleep, and that was the last time I ever heard my mother's voice."

I started at that. He smiled bitterly.

"Three days later, my dad picked me up from school and we drove, but not for home. Instead, we drove for hours to Ichabod, Montana. I was maybe...six or seven at the time, too young to really understand it, or so I thought. I was tired and hungry, and I really needed to go to the bathroom. But my dad...I remember there was such a worried look in his eyes that I never saw before, and so I didn't ask questions.

"We arrived in Ichabod close to sunset. It was the only time I was ever there, but it was enough."

We were passing under that tree tunnel I mentioned before. I watched the shadows pass over his face, one after the other, as he spoke.

"You ever see an abandoned town, Jim? It's buildings standing vacant, looking like they haven't seen the wet end of a paintbrush in years. It's cars abandoned on the side of the road for no good reason that you can see. It's windows, dark and empty, staring out on empty streets, and when you look inside all you see is darkness and the absence of any life that may have once been."

"That's awfully poetic," I joked, but he didn't hear me by this point; he was lost in the land of his memories.

"We stopped at this crossroads, and we stood there in pitch black, no streetlights were on. My dad...he got out and he...he took me with him. And we walked down this dark street, with the only light coming from our car's high beams. He's calling out Mom's name and I'm clinging onto his hand for dear life.

"We stopped at this crossroads, and we stood there in the dark. He kept calling her name and his voice just echoed down the street. No one ever answered. We never saw anyone while we were there. All we were met with was that awful, final silence."

He asked for another cigarette, and I gave it. He lit it and drummed his fingers on the steering wheel. "But it was that walk back that always stuck with me. As we were walking back to the car, I looked up at those windows and I felt...eyes. Watching us. Watching *me*. Suddenly this town didn't feel abandoned. It felt like they were all in those windows, watching me. Waiting for us to leave so they could return to their crypt of a city."

He smoked in silence. I took his story with a healthy degree of skepticism. I didn't believe much in paranormal happenings – Kent changed that for the most part – and I believed that a seven-year-old in a dead town could envision the eyes of the dead staring down at him.

"And your mom?" I asked.

He shrugged. "I suppose it's possible she ran off with some secret lover and started a new life. I'm not so far down the conspiracy hole that I wouldn't accept that as a possibility."

"But you don't think so."

"No." He pitched his second cigarette. "No, I think she found what she was looking for. And it took her."

I didn't ask what "it" was. I didn't really want to know.

We were getting closer to Kent, and I was starting to get nervous. The moment of truth was right around the corner. Either we'd solve the mystery...or it would live to spook another day.

"You think what happened in Ichabod is happening in Kent?" I asked.

"All I know for sure is that it has become too easy for a town to disappear," was his answer. "And that's enough to make me worried."

We were rounding the bend, and just up ahead I could see the lights of the town. My heart beat faster as Webster punched the gas to speed us up. We got closer and closer...and then my heart plummeted in my chest when I saw the town sign with "Welcome to Bangor!" stamped on in big, red, painted letters.

Webster slammed on the brakes and the car screeched to a halt. We sat there, dumbfounded, staring at the sign, expecting it to pull a "Gotcha!" and change its words to what they were supposed to be. Knowing that they wouldn't.

We had taken no detours. The road never split off. There was no way we could have gotten turned around. And yet somehow, we had found ourselves right back where we had started.

Just like Trigger had said.

My mouth was open, slack jawed. I tried to say something, anything, but no words would come out. Webster put his head on the steering wheel and kept it there for a long, long time.

And that's the story of our trip to Kent.

Some ride, huh?

# 12

"Wait, wait," the girl said, holding her hand up. "I'm sorry, you're losing me."

The old man grinned. He had expected this. "Which part?"

"This Ichabod thing. Like, now there's two cities with the same disappearing act? I didn't read anything about it in my research."

"You wouldn't," he said, "because Web and I never reported it to the Kent Committee. And I didn't say they were the exact same disappearing act."

"It sure sounds like it. I mean-"

"Settle down." He held his hand up. "Let's back up. After everything was over, I did investigate Ichabod, Montana. It was a real town at one point, a mining town, and it was finally torn down back in '98. At the time of the exodus, it housed about eleven thousand people."

"So then why-"

"Never explained. To start, though, not everyone from that town went missing in the literal sense. Some were found in different parts of the country, living their ordinary lives. One guy was found fishing on the Alaskan coast, another one was a security guard in a Florida shopping mall. One woman was even working as a secretary to a senator from Wyoming. A reporter tracked them all down and asked them why they left."

"And...what did they say?"

The old man shrugged. "Some didn't even answer. Others said they just decided to leave. Simple as that."

"All of them?"

"Just the ones that they found, remember. There were a lot more that were never found and never appeared again."

"But why? Where did they go? How do that many people just disappear without a trace?"

He shrugged. "People disappear a lot more often than you think. All over the world. Think of all those urban legends: The Bermuda Triangle, Mesa Verde, Roanoke, the Bennington Triangle, the Devil's Sea, so on and so forth. It happens all the time. People will just drop off the face of the Earth, sometimes right in front of witnesses. Why? Hell, probably for the same reason people believe the Loch Ness Monster and Bigfoot exist. They just do. And New England is one of the biggest examples of unexplained mysteries. This *is* Lovecraft territory, after all.

"About five years ago, I was near Portland for my granddaughter's wedding. Driving along our route, we passed house after house after house that were clearly long abandoned. I watched all those houses and wondered where their owners were, what had happened to them. I couldn't think of any reason why they'd all stay deserted like that. They just were."

"My God," the girl whispered, looking horrified.

"All over the world, people drop out of sight at an average of a couple thousand a year. Most of them are considered runaways. I imagine a lot of them even are."

He signaled for the waitress to bring the next round of drinks over. The Bingo game was inching closer to its climax; all that remained were the dozen or so who were scoring the highest, all with their eyes on the prize.

He leaned in again, and she leaned in with him. The smell of root beer was so strong that it was almost paralyzing, but once again, she didn't back away.

"But I'll tell you something else about that trip," he went on. "At the end of the reception, my daughter-in-law fell and broke her wrist. It was rainy and she had had a bit too much to drink, and y'know, shit happens. Anyway, we took her to the hospital in Portland, and we spent the night in the heart of the city. I'll tell you, I've been in a lot of big cities at night – Boston, Brooklyn, Austin, Savannah, Columbia, the list goes on – and I have never felt unsafe in any of them except for Portland. It's not that they have a high crime rate, although we saw plenty of hoodlums outside of that 7-Eleven. No, Portland just had a...a *vibe* to it. A vibe that says that although it *looks* pleasant and friendly, it *could* get plenty mean if it wanted to, you betcha. Wouldn't even have to try. Like there's a darkness hiding just underneath the surface, waiting for the right moment to sink its teeth in."

He sat back as the new round of drinks came in. "I didn't used to think that way, but after Webster's confession on that drive, I think about those things more. It sounds ridiculous, but I'm older now, and I keep a very open mind. And you'd be wise to do the same."

She nodded slowly. Then she took a sip from her drink. Some of it spilled down her chin, and she mopped her shirt off before the stains came in. That broke the tension for the moment, but no more than that.

The old man continued his story.

# 13

On the fifth day, it snowed. A surprise cold front came overnight, and that morning Bangor woke up to a thick blanket of snow on its rooftops and frosting on the car windshields. It was too wet to do much with, but it was a nice, pleasant surprise to the residents, even if it did catch the plows by surprise. Maine winters are brutal, but this snowfall was a light one.

But of course, in Kent, if it could get worse, it would. We fielded about fifty calls that day that told us their story: they got snow, all right. A lot of it.

Shortly after dawn, the light in the sky went haywire, going from purple to red to blue to yellow and so on and so on. The snow fell and stuck to everything. Winds whipped up to thirty miles per hour at the least. Snow built up by a foot in under an hour. Cars couldn't move, and people couldn't open their doors without an avalanche falling into their front halls. By noon, according to the people there, the town was blanketed under a sea of white, unable to do much of anything.

We probably would have gotten even more calls, except that was the day we lost contact with Kent.

At one thirty-five, the phones stopped ringing, and we couldn't call in. The storm, we figured, had knocked out the powerlines. That was the official reason, and the likely one, but I don't think it was the only one.

The last call we got out of Kent that day was from Dan Billings, the town postmaster, a man who was known to spin more than a couple of yarns. Stugley was the one who answered that call, and I'll tell ya, I got a smidge of satisfaction seeing him looking like he was contemplating drinking paint thinner.

According to Stugley, Dan was going on and on about the snow when he abruptly stopped. Stugley, whose mind had drifted probably to that waitress at Denny's with the nice legs that he had always eyed, was brought back to the present by the pause.

"Dan? You still there?"

"Wait a sec," Dan said, and the distracted tone of his voice made Stugley alert.

There was a moment's pause. Then Dan said, "I see something...coming out of the cornfield, through the snow...I think i-"

Then the line went dead.

"Hello? Dan? Dan?" Stugley hit the receiver repeatedly. "Dan? Hello?"

He tried calling back, but all he got was the operator telling him that service in Kent had been cut off. We tried a few other numbers, all with the same result. No one was calling in, and no one could call out.

Well, lemme tell ya, after four whole days of utter mayhem – four and a half, at that point – to suddenly go from that to complete silence, it was fucking *spooky*. We weren't used to things being peaceful after the week we had gone through. I actually *missed* the noise; can you believe that? But worse than that, it meant that we were now completely in the dark regarding Kent instead of just partially in the dark. A bomb could have gone off downtown and we would not have known it.

For the third time that week, Webster called Orono for their helicopter. This time, it was a firm no. The visibility was too bad, was one reason; that after two previous attempts which yielded no results, they didn't see a point to it, was the other.

Webby, he flipped. Fully flipped. He picked the phone up off his desk and threw it against the wall, ripping the cord out of the wall, it narrowly missed Trigger's head as he came back with coffee; the phone exploded against the wall was more than enough to make him drop his mug, it shattering against the hard marble floor.

"Jesus *Christ*!" cried Trigger, clutching his chest. "What the f-"

Web swung his hands across his desk and brushed everything on the surface onto the floor. We all gaped at him as he kicked his chair over, and I mean he kicked that son of a bitch so hard he broke one of the back beams clean off it. It would've been impressive if it hadn't been so scary.

He raged for a full minute before Chief Jennings and two others managed to restrain him and bring him to an isolation room, where he spent the next three hours stewing in frustration and agony at his inability to do more.

Frank and I looked at each other, both of our expressions tired and fearful.

"What do we do now?" I asked, but I already knew the answer.

Frank lit a cigarette and shrugged.

"Nothing," he said. "Wait."

The rest of that day, and most of the sixth day, were completely silent. We addressed a car accident on Sixth Avenue, and a domestic dispute in front of the LaVerdiere's, but other than that, it was like the clock had run back to before this whole disaster began. It was almost peaceful.

Webster was antsy the whole day, snapping at anyone who interrupted his train of thought. We all worried about him, but we didn't know what to do, so in the end, we did nothing.

# 14

The old man's face suddenly grew dark. He reached for his root beer, and accidentally knocked it over with a shaking hand. It fell to the floor and shattered.

"Shit!" he said. He signaled to the waitress for assistance.

The girl watched all of this with sudden alarm. He didn't look at her at all as he directed the waitress on the mess, and then talked pleasantly as she left to get him some water. The sudden shift in his demeanor frightened her a little. Fleetingly she wondered if it was too late to call it for the night, say she didn't want to hear anymore. She suddenly wasn't sure she wanted to know the rest.

When he turned back to her, he saw her looking expectantly at him, and his face regained its grim attire. The girl waited patiently for him to continue. When he did, his voice, which had gotten so scratchy from the hour and a half of talking, sounded soft, almost weak.

"The last call that ever came out of Kent came towards the end of the sixth day, at eleven thirty-six. I was the one who answered it, and I remember every word." He stared down at the table; his eyes were already lost in the past. "God help me, I remember every one."

# 15

It was quiet that night. Most of the staff had gone home for the night; in our office, all that was left were the five of us that had started that week off. Frank was taking a nap in his seat, Stugley and Trigger were playing rummy on Trigger's desk, a bottle of Jameson between them with a couple of shot glasses next to it, and Webster was trying to do the daily crossword puzzle, but I could tell his heart wasn't really into it.

I was pitching paper clips into a cup and glancing over at Webby to make sure he wasn't going to pitch another fit. My worries about my partner were hitting an all-time high, and I was remembering his story from the other night, the empty town where his mother had disappeared. Amazing how little that tale had etched into Webster's features until this case. Now I was wondering if he'd ever be the same again.

I was about to say something to try and get his mind of it when the phone on my desk rang. All our heads picked up – Frank snapped out of his nap instantly – and looked at it; I think we all had phone PTSD by this point. I looked each one of them in the eye – Web held my gaze the longest – and then I picked the phone up to the worst nightmare of my life.

"Bangor Police Station," I said.

There was no answer. On the other end, I could hear heavy breathing that sounded muffled against one's cupped palm. I gulped, and even before she said it, I knew where this was coming from.

"Hello? Is anyone there?"

"*Help me.*"

It was a woman's voice, soft and scared and sounding impossibly young. My blood ran so cold that I felt like I was being submerged in the deep Atlantic Ocean.

"Ma'am, who am I speaking with?" I asked, doing everything I can to keep my voice steady and level. The others picked up on it, though; Webster got up from his desk and crossed over to mine.

"Help me, please God help me."

"Ma'am, calm down. Who am I speaking with?"

"Amy...Amy Schumacher...please, you have to help me."

"We will, we will. Just tell us what's happening."

There was a sob, then silence, and then: "They came back..."

I licked my lips as the others gathered around as well. "Who came back, ma'am?"

"Everyone...they came in from the woods, through the snow and ice...we thought they'd returned home, so we went out to greet them-"

There was a long pause, broken only with punctured breathing. The others were watching me, but I didn't even register them. At that moment, it was just me and the girl on the phone; everyone else might as well have been on Mars.

Then she said, "My little brother and sister...they came to live with me after our parents passed. They're good kids, but they don't...they don't always listen to me, you know? I told them not to play outside near the woods, not with all the craziness, but they just wanted to go outside..."

"Ma'am, you're losing me. Come back. You said everyone came back but who-"

"*Everyone!*" she hissed, loud enough to be heard by me but not for where she was; she sounded like she was trying hard to keep anyone on her end from hearing her. "The children, all the people who left town over the last few days, they've come back and they're...they're hunting for the rest of us!"

Any other time before all this, I would have thought I was being pranked with an Alfred Hitchcock script, but after the week we had gone through, I felt all the color drain from my face. An image of Ernest Lanslow shuffling through the snow like a zombie, face blue and frozen, eyes glazed over with that foggy look of the dead, filled my mind like a movie reel. Next, I imagined all those kids out there, looking and acting the same. The idea alone was enough to drive one mad.

"We thought they had found their way home," Amy continued, and she was sobbing softly into the phone now. "Some went out to greet them, and the kids...they descended upon them. One or two let out a scream before they...and then when they were done, they went after the rest of us. One or two houses opened their doors, and...all we heard after was screams. Everyone else is locked up. I haven't talked to anyone in almost twenty-four hours, but I *hear* them, I hear them moving around out there-"

"Do you hear them now?" I asked.

"No...once night fell, I barricaded myself in my bedroom closet. I don't know how many people are left-"

There was a sudden loud smashing of glass on her end that made me jump in my chair. Web started for me, but I held my hand up.

"Ma'am? Are you alright?"

The breathing on the other end grew heavier.

"Oh my God," she whispered. "Something just came inside."

"Stay quiet and stay in the closet."

"What's happening?" Trigger asked, but Frank shushed him. Just as well; by that point I was so lost in the situation that a herd of oxen couldn't have taken me out of it.

For the longest time, there was nothing on the other end except her breathing. I was trembling, but I kept my hand as steady as I could. Every now and again I would glance at Webster and see his pale, intense face staring back at me.

I didn't say anything, though, because that girl needed my undivided attention. Even if we were separated by miles and by whatever fucking God awful barrier was cutting them off from us, she and I were in this together. That might sound dramatic, but you gotta understand that with any kind of home invasion, that person on the other end of the 9-1-1 call is your guardian angel. They're your only lifeline to the outside world. Your problem is their problem. And there was no way I was leaving this girl alone, no matter what happened.

Those minutes before it happened were some of the most nerve-wracking of my life. With no visuals to look at, all I had were the sounds on the phone and my own mind to fill in the blanks. Somehow, that was worse. It's like I told you earlier. The mind alone makes worse horror than any jump scare.

After what felt like eternity, I heard a door creak open, and Amy's breath hitched. Then I heard voices, different voices...and the sound of them caused my mouth to dry up and my balls to shrivel up. Sorry for the imagery, but it's the truth.

It was a boy and a girl, both maybe nine or ten, but there was...there was nothing human about them. Nothing. They were good imitations, but they lacked any warmth or humanity that they would normally have. They sounded hollowed out and empty, like what I imagine a ventriloquist dummy would sound like if it could talk on its own. If that was just what they talked like, I thank God every day that I never saw what they looked like. I may have ended up killing myself if I had.

"*Sissy,*" the boy voice said. "*Sissy, are you in here?*"

"*It's us, Sissy,*" the girl followed with. "*It's us, we've come home.*"

"*Where are you, Sissy? Why won't you come see us?*"

"*We just want to play.*"

"*To play, just like we used to.*"

"*We're sorry we worried you.*"

"*But we have such things to show you.*"

"*Such wonderful things.*"

"*Come out, come out, Sissy.*"

"*So we can all be together again.*" The girl ended her sentence with a hollow sigh.

"Stay completely still," I said, as quietly as I could muster.

For a moment, I thought that maybe she could wait them out and pull through. Then she let out an audible, high-pitched gasp that was half-muffled against her hand. It was that gasp; I'm convinced of that. It was that gasp that got her killed.

The last words I ever heard her say was, "*Oh my God their EYES!*"

I never got the chance to respond, because almost immediately there was a loud BANG and a loud, almost animalistic sounding voice said, with absolute, unbridled glee:

"FOUND YOU!"

And that's when she started screaming, and...and...

The old man suddenly started breathing heavily. The girl shot up, knocking her chair over loud enough that all the remaining patrons turned to look at them. The Bingo game, in its final round, paused for the first time that night on their account, the host looking anxious and concerned, likely wondering if they were going to have to end the night with an ambulance visit.

"Are you okay?" The girl asked him.

The old man tried to speak, but the words choked in his throat. She looked up at the staff.

"Somebody get some help over here!" She cried out.

But the old man held his hand up and waved them away.

"I'm fine, I'm fine," he choked out. "I'm sorry, I just...I need a minute."

The girl looked anxiously at him. The staff hovered nearby for a moment until they were sure the old man wasn't having a heart attack.

Gradually he got his breathing under control. The Bingo game resumed, somewhat hesitantly. The staff resumed their jobs, although every so often they glanced over just in case.

He got his breathing under control and urged the girl to sit back down. She picked her chair back up and did so, though the palpable concern was still playing in her face. The old man suddenly looked older, more tired, and infinitely more sad. There were tears in his eyes as he spoke again.

"If you've ever heard a person scream for their life," he said, "then you know. If you haven't, then you don't. You can't. There are no words to explain the pure terror in a person's screams when they are faced with the reality that their number is up. No comparisons I make can help you hear the shrill, blood-chilling noise that pierces your eardrums and bounces around in your head for long after it's done. I listened to that woman scream her lungs empty for ten of the worst seconds of my life...and I never, ever, ever, I eat on it, I sleep on it, I *dream* on it...I *never* forgot her screams. There are days, even now, where I'll be sitting in silence or doing some mundane task, and out of nowhere I'll be back in that office that night and I'll hear those screams again.

"That's my scar right there. That's my Ichabod, Montana. Those screams."

They only went for ten seconds, and then the line went dead for the last time.

I placed the phone on the cradle with a hand that shook so bad it almost knocked the damn thing off my desk. The others stared at me with eyes full of fear.

"We need to go to Kent," I said, standing up. "We need to go right now. I don't care if it just keeps spitting us out back in Bangor, we have to *try!*"

Stugley immediately agreed. That's the one thing I will always give that bastard credit for: for all the shit he talked, he had the balls to back it up. Frank agreed to come, arthritis be damned, and after a moment's hesitation, Trigger agreed too. I looked at Webster, and we locked eyes for a solid moment, but I never for a second doubted his resolve. Especially not after our trip the other night.

He nodded. "Let's go. We'll drive until we either break through or we run out of gas."

As it turned out, that wasn't necessary.

I said at the start that Kent was nothing but a crater. And that's true; if you go there today, you'll find no sign of any town there. But there was one trip into the town before it disappeared. Just one.

# 16

The old man took a sip of water and exhaled deeply. He smiled.

"When you're a young man," he said softly, "you act a lot on impulse. Young men in particular have a fascination with playing the hero, most often when there's a lady involved. It's only when you've grown and walked around the world a while longer that you realize that a lot of that perceived heroism is mostly pride and bravado. They think only they can save the day, but only later realize that the day has usually been decided before they even left their home.

"We went out to Kent that night with the intention of saving those people, but even we didn't comprehend that their fate had been sealed long before that night, and that whole week had just been us parading around pretending to be doing anything important. Things had been decided before we had even gotten that first call; how else do you explain the cutoff road and seeming inobservance from the air?"

The girl didn't answer, didn't even shrug her shoulders. She stared with tense eyes, hanging on his every word. She was lost in the story now, he knew; this was the part of the story she had sought him out for. Now that she was here, he wondered if she was regretting doing so.

He smiled again, but his smile was a wistful one.

"If we hadn't gone to Kent that night, if we had waited until morning when it would have been too late, would it have made any difference? I wonder that a lot, too. If we had chosen to stay at the station instead of going out into the unknown, who knows? Maybe everything afterwards might have been different. Maybe Webster and Stugley and Trigger...maybe they'd even still be alive today..."

Her eyes went wide. "You mean they-"

"Hmm?" He looked up, saw her expression, and chuckled. "Oh, no, they weren't killed on this trip. Don't worry, no one dies in my story, apart from the people in Kent...and you know, even now, after all this time, I'm still not convinced those people actually died. Don't ask me why I think that, it's just...a feeling I've always had.

"But it is true that, of the five of us that started that week answering phone calls, I'm the only one who is still alive. And a part of it, I'm sure, is because of that trip. It put its hold on us and it followed us for all our lives, because we were the only ones who walked into that place and walked back out. How could we have known that it wouldn't just let us leave?

"You don't consider that when you're younger. The consequences. You just don't. And as we grow up, it's our elder selves that have to deal with them."

# 17

We took two squad cars and loaded ourselves to the nines with guns and ammo. No relief mission this time. This time we were going hunting.

I'll spare you the car trip and the conversations that occurred; I already covered them before, and little of it was different. On the contrary, it was like a regular trip out that we would have taken before. Even the tree tunnel almost seemed back to normal, back to the icy winter wonderland that just a few days ago was so damp and dreary. Passing that to the Kent entrance made the hairs on my arm stand on end. Even the fuckin' trees seemed haunted.

At that point we were fully expecting to see the sign for Bangor, so you can imagine our shock when the sign to welcome us to Kent loomed out from the dark. It was past midnight by then. I guess Kent's horse and carriage finally turned back into four mice and a pumpkin.

We had to stop right on the edge of town on account of the snow that was built up so much it was impassible. We got out of the car, grabbed our weapons, and began the trudge. The snow was up to our waists, and in our haste, we had forgotten shovels and snow clothes. I swear to ya, I was numb from the waist down for three days afterwards.

I think I expected the town to be nothing but a pile of ashes by this point, but aside from being buried under two feet of snow, the town looked no different than it ever had, with one major difference: there wasn't a single light on. Not even a streetlight. Kent was covered in a blanket of darkness as well as a blanket of snow.

We walked through the snow single file, the leader breaking the path through the snow, the other two shining the lights to guide the leader alone. Every so often, we'd switch off; the guy at the front would move to the back of the line, and the man behind them would move to the back of the line and catch some rest. And we'd repeat that again and again.

Well, that was the plan, but we didn't get far into the order before Frank started to go down. Cold weather is hell on arthritis, and at sixty-two he wasn't exactly a spring chicken anymore. That plus the lack of snow gear, and he was in a bad state before we even got two blocks. When it was his turn to front, he made it three steps before he fell to his knees.

"I'm locking up bad," he said, and that made me nervous. It was out of character for him to complain.

We were in front of this red house, and figured it was as good as any to set up an outpost. We moved to the door, and Webster and Trigger kicked it open.

"Police!" Webster shouted. "Anyone inside, say something!"

There was no answer.

We moved Frank to the living room. There were a couple logs in the fireplace, and some newspapers around. Stugley put the paper in the fireplace on top of the logs and used his lighter to get a fire going.

"Wood's not great, but it'll burn," he said, standing up. "Dunno for how long, though. We should look around for some more material to keep the fire going."

The fire had illuminated enough of the living room that I could flash my light around and look for...hell, I don't know. Blood? Signs of a struggle? Any evidence of an ordinary case, even though even I knew that all pretense of this being an ordinary case was long gone? I couldn't have told you, except that I was a cop, and investigation was part of my job.

The house we were in was the small, cozy get-up your grandmother's house might have. A small lavender throw rug rested on the blue carpet, underneath a small mahogany coffee table with a vase and two coasters. The chair was peach-colored, cushioned, with sky-blue pillows resting against the arm rests. There was a TV across from a red couch, one of those older boxes with antennas for reception (1960, remember), and behind it on the windowsill was a potted plant. Pictures aligned a small table, and pictures and paintings adorned the bird-and-flower wallpaper that covered the walls.

Completely unremarkable, was what I thought as I shone my light around the room and took it all in. wouldn't know anything was wrong from the look of it. It just looked like Grammy had stepped out for a spell and left everything as it was.

But...something was off. There was something not right. And all I had to do was look closer, and I could see it.

The wallpaper's color was faded, muted. None of it was tearing, but it hadn't been maintained in what must have been years. The tables, I noticed, all had a fine layer of dust on the surfaces, and dust had settled on the picture frames so much that you could barely make out the faces. There were cobwebs stretching out from under the lampshades, and more were hanging from the windowsill. The TV screen was so dusty you couldn't watch anything on it even if the reception was good.

But it wasn't just the neglect of the room. It was the *age*, you see? It was the stale taste of the air and the way the dust settled on your tongue. It was like what I imagine opening an Egyptian tomb was like, but without the stench of death permeating. Somehow, a house that had been occupied only days or even hours beforehand, now looked as though it hadn't been touched in months or even years.

I called the others over and showed them my findings. I watched the color drained from Webster's face as his mind made the connection. The others had grasped it as well.

"Alright...alright, we don't know anything for sure yet," said Stugley. "This house could've been abandoned for a long time before all this. Let's check the others before we jump to any conclusions. Alright?"

He was keeping it together, and for once I agreed with him. I looked at Webster for confirmation and nudged him when he didn't respond. He started, and then shook his head clear.

"Yeah...okay, LaRose, you stay here with Frank and try to see what else you can find. Stugley, O'Sullivan, you're with me."

No one gave any argument. I think Trigger was glad he didn't have to go back out there, and I imagine the bolt-action rifle he was carrying made him feel even better about staying put. Frank looked annoyed, but he didn't argue; he knew when he'd hit his limit. He got himself situated on the couch in front of the fire while the three of us went back out on our search.

How do I explain it, that trip down the dark, snowy roads of Kent? How do I talk about the awful silence that lingered like a bad stench? It was easy to talk about Ichabod 'cuz all I had to do was tell Web's story, but it's harder to explain when it's my turn. Because I don't have the words, you see? I don't know the words to describe that kind of crushing emptiness that I felt there.

What I will tell you is that it was so quiet in that town that if you dropped a pin on a solid surface, you'd hear it clear over in the next county. It was the sound of our feet crunching snow, and our heavy breathing, and that was it. Not even in the middle of the deep woods have I ever experienced such a definite quiet such as that, either before that night or after it. If you've never experienced something like that, then there's no way you can know. Because it's loneliness, crushing loneliness...but there was also something more, hidden underneath.

It was the way I would flash my light around and think I saw something move just on the edge of it but couldn't quite catch it. It was the way we would stop to get our bearings, and I could just swear that I could hear snow crunching nearby, but when I'd turn to look, I'd find no one there. It was the way the houses seemed empty, and at the same time felt like everyone was still inside, standing at the windows, watching us as we tried to find them, a never-ending game of cat and mouse.

No embellishment. No exaggeration. That's what I felt then, and that's what I feel now.

After a time – I have no way of remembering how long – we investigated another house. Again, we started by kicking in the door and announcing ourselves. Again, we were met with that awful silence. We flashed lights around and checked the surroundings and were dismayed to find that the status of this house was the exact same as the one before: old, abandoned, and looking like it hadn't been cleaned in years.

Webster stared at a dusty picture of a family of five: father, mother, two girls and a boy, and a little Pomeranian at their feet. All of them looked happy, none of them showing any indication of what was to come. He shook his head.

"This is unbelievable," he said softly. "Absolutely unbelievable."

"This is spooky as shit," Stugley groaned. "How the hell did they all get cleared out of here so *fast*? Hell, how did they clear out at *all*? Snow's practically up to our tits, how the hell did any of them get out of their homes? And without leaving tracks? Makes no sense!"

I peeked out the window. The black stared back at me, which is about as ridiculous as it sounds, but if you've never been alone in a dark town like that, you start to feel like the dark itself is watching you. The lack of streetlights or any house lights were spooking me out.

"Okay...okay." Webster turned to us. "I'll stay here and look around a little more, see if I can find anyone. You two check out the next house over and see if you can find anyone there."

Stugley nodded, but I said, "You sure you want to be here by yourself, Web?"

"I'll be fine. Get going."

His response was harsh, disconnected from us. Already his mind was on trying to find a survivor in this retched place. I took Stugley and left, not without reservation. It was too much like a horror movie, splitting us up like that, Webby going off on his own. I didn't like it one bit, but the fact was splitting up so multiple officers could investigate different sections was more efficient than everyone gathered in one spot in the whole town.

We stepped out and turned onto the next house, which was on the opposite side of the road at a four-way intersection. I took this time to raise Trigger on the radio.

"How's it going over there, Trig?" I asked.

"Surviving," came his answer a moment later. "Frank is still on the couch. I've been keeping the fire going best I can, but he's not doing too good. When are you guys coming back?"

"We're gonna check one or two more houses and then I think we'll make our way back to you. Have you checked out any more of the house?"

"Just the kitchen. Same condition as the living room. Dust and cobwebs everywhere. There's an English muffin on the counter that's so molded over I almost gagged. Is it the same in the other houses?"

"We only checked one so far, but yeah. Same story. We're gonna see how the next one looks. If it's the same there as well, then I think it's safe to say the whole town is like this."

"Jesus Christ, *how?*"

"Let's just get through the rest of this. We can debate the how and why later. I'll radio you when we're wrapping up."

"Alrighty. Good luck, Jim."

"You too, Trig."

I clipped my walkie back to my belt and followed Stugley to the next house. Unlike the other houses, this one's door was wide open, and I could see one of the front windows smashed in. I didn't catch the name on the mailbox, but suddenly, I knew. Don't ask me how. I chalk it up to intuition. You don't get to be a good cop without it.

I drew my gun again. Stugley saw it and drew his.

"We expecting trouble?" he asked me.

"I think this is the house that girl was calling from," I answered. "The one that got us out here."

"Shit. You think whatever got her is still in there?"

"If they are, they're in for a rough surprise."

He smiled. "I like the sound of that."

We entered the door, guns drawn. Despite the scene in the front yard, the inside was remarkably untouched. No furniture overturned, no picture frames askew, no broken glass aside from the one window. There were no footprints on the carpet, nor were there any leading up to the upstairs.

I looked at Stugley and nodded my head towards the kitchen, wordlessly telling him to check downstairs while I went up. He nodded and pulled out his flashlight, pressing forward into the dark. I went upstairs slowly, taking my time. If anyone was still in there, it was possible they knew we had arrived. I wasn't about to rush headlong into my death.

When I reached the landing, I peeked my head out for a quick look before I made the turn. The hallway was mostly barren, save for a table with more picture frames on it. The frames had pictures of a red-haired freckled woman smiling with a pair of little red-haired tykes with her. All three of them looked happy and healthy and impossibly young. I tried not to focus on them too much.

At the end of the hall was a doorway that was wide open. I slowly peered in, gun ready, fingering the trigger in case this was the moment to pull it. It wasn't. The room was empty, but unlike the rest of the house, it was in total bedlam. The bedsheets had been ripped off, the pillows had been torn open and feathers littered the area; it looked like two swans had gotten into a helluva fight. The burrow was turned over, and as I looked under, I saw that the mirror had been smashed and broken glass rested under it. Clothes had been thrown in disarray from the closet door, which was wide open...and here, at the entrance to this door, was the only spots of blood I found that entire night.

I bent down and investigated best I could. There was a big oval stain, like someone had dumped a pitcher of Kool-Aid on the floor. There were smaller splatters on the doorframe and the door itself. There was no smear, though; no line leading out of the closet. Whatever had happened here had begun and ended right at this spot...and then they had just disappeared.

Which sounded impossible, of course, but there was plenty of that to go around at this point.

But even the state of the room looked old, like it had been a while since whatever happened here had happened. Even the blood was more of a brown color than a red, a sign that it had set into the carpet a long time ago...and just *how* was that possible? I had talked to this girl not an hour ago, yet it looked as if this mess was five years old at least.

I thought of Trigger's car, of the time that still showed it being four hours behind what it actually was. Time seemed to work differently with this phenomenon, we knew that at the beginning of the week, but we hadn't considered the possibility that Kent itself was in accelerated time. Once I had entertained that thought, another more horrifying one occurred: exactly how long had Kent been dealing with this? For us it was a week, but who knows how long it was in Kent's time. A month? A year? Ten? I didn't know. And I never would know.

Well, you know the saying: once is happenstance, twice is coincidence, but three times is enemy action. It was all but confirmed for me now that whatever happened here was long over.

Suddenly, Webster came on the radio. I just about jumped out of my damn skin when his voice shot out through the quiet.

"Survivor found! Survivor found! I need both of you back here now!"

I turned and booked it down the stairs, taking them two at a time, as Stugley came barreling out of the kitchen. We came out the front door and back across the street, using the path we had cleared before to get there faster.

Webster appeared in the front entryway just as we arrived, and damn if we didn't almost run directly into him.

"I was inspecting upstairs, and I found him hiding in the pantry," he explained. "A little boy. He was huddled up in a ball, looked scared to death."

"Is he hurt?" I asked.

"Don't know. Help me move him."

The three of us bolted up the stairs, putting our guns back in their holsters and allowing the lights to lead our way. This upstairs floor was one of those open floor plan kind of deals, no narrow hallway, with multiple doors. Webby lead us to one at the far end, which looked like a master bedroom. Outside it was a small pantry with the door open.

I shone my light to the bottom of the pantry. There was a blanket on the floor, but no kid on top of it.

"Uh, Web?" I turned to him. His face had gone ghostly pale.

"No no no..." He looked around, then started pulling things out of the pantry and throwing them to the floor. "He was *here*, goddammit! He was *right here*!"

Stugley and I exchanged glances. You'd probably guess that we thought he had finally lost it. Well, we didn't. After what we had seen and heard that night, if Web was losing it then we were certainly losing it too. We were in a town that was defying logic, so if Web said he saw a kid there, then we believed him. What we couldn't figure out was how the kid could have gotten by him when he was blocking the stairwell when we got in.

I checked inside the pantry again. The blanket on the bottom was pink and slightly ruffled...and, as I inspect closer, had some old clumps of dirt that resembled the underside of a child's shoe.

I showed the other two. Neither could say anything. I mean what *could* you say to that? If this was today, we'd probably realize that this kid had blinked in and out of our timeline like a hologram. Months later I did my own research into what Webby might have seen. That boy might have sat there at the time when the town was destroyed, and Webster might have seen what they call an echo of it. For a brief moment the timelines merged or something like that and Webster got to see the boy that was already long gone before we'd even gotten there, and he was gone again by the time we had arrived to save him.

That's the best way I know how to explain it. I have no idea if I'm right or not, so take that with a grain of salt.

I put my hand on my friend's shoulder. Stugley just stood there idly, unsure how to proceed.

"I don't understand," said Webster helplessly. "I don't understand any of it."

"You didn't understand Ichabod, Montana either," I told him. "That didn't matter. It still was what it was."

He looked at me, startled. I shrugged. Stugley looked back and forth between us, stuck somewhere between confused and apprehensive.

"What do you want to do, Web?" he asked.

Webster didn't answer him right away. After a moment, Stugley spoke again.

"Look, why don't we head back to the station, get more guys and supplies, and come b ack out at first light. Alright? Maybe get some sleep while we're at it."

"Getting scared on me, Stugs?" Webster asked, an almost taunting sound to his voice that was so unlike him that I stared at him in shock.

"Fuck scared. I'm pointing out the facts. It's dark, it's freezing, Frank's already going down, and I don't see much point in wandering around a dead town looking for people that aren't here."

"I'm telling you, he was-"

"*There's no one here*, Web! I've never seen a deader town in my life!"

"*Guys*!" I snapped. My head was starting to pound, part from the cold and the dusty air, part from the volume of the argument. "Stugley's right, Pete. Five of us aren't going to accomplish much with the snow this high, especially with one of us too weak to move. Let's go back, rest, regroup, and then come back with reinforcements. The town will still be here when we get back."

On that last note, I turned out to be dead wrong. Not that I had any way of knowing that in the moment. But it was enough for Webster, who finally conceded to us.

The trip back wasn't as grueling as the one forward, mostly because we had already cut a clear path through the snow. We met up with the other two – Frank was in a lot of pain by this point, he needed two of us to help him back to the cars – and made our exit. Nothing stopped us. We made it back to the cars in one piece.

I helped Frank into the back of the first car, and then Webster and I got into the second. We waited until the others had pulled out and taken off, and then Webster threw us in gear. We had to back up before we could go forward, and when we did, I took one last look at the empty town behind us, and I saw...

Again, the old man stopped in the middle of his tale. There was no panic attack this time, no heavy breathing, but he suddenly just stared off into nothing. He took a long drink from his water and wiped his mouth with his sleeve. The girl was looking concerned again.

"What's wrong?" she asked.

He opened his mouth again, paused, closed it, paused again, then opened his mouth again.

"Nothing," he said, and took another sip. "Just...it's fine. I just wanted to finish this drink up."

She continued to stare at him, and he knew she didn't buy it. He placed his now empty glass down.

"You have to understand," he said slowly, his eyes looking at her pleadingly. "I've never told anyone this part. Not the committee, not the press, not my wife. Webster never even knew what I saw. If I had said anything, it probably would have been the final straw that would've thrown me into the wacky shack. I had fully intended to take it with me to the grave."

"Oh..." she gulped and nodded. "Okay, that's fine, we can skip it if it'll make you more comfortable-"

"No, that's not it, that's...what I'm trying to tell you is, you've been a great listener through all this. And I don't have too many years left to me, so...so I might as well pass that memory on to someone else. Let them carry that burden. Do you think you can be the one to handle that?"

They stared at each other for a long time, and in that moment, nothing else mattered. Not the waiters, not the Bingo game, nothing. All that mattered was the two people at the table, and the decision on if this girl was going to carry the burden of memory to an event that no one wanted to remember. What happened next would determine everything.

She nodded. There was a pause. She nodded again.

"Okay," he said, nodding back. "Then here it is. What ended the whole affair for me."

As we were backing up, I looked behind me at that empty town...and I saw figures, standing at the edge of the town. Three of them; one tall one and two small ones. The small ones were holding the hands of the large one, and in the other hand of one of them hung a raggedy-looking doll. They were staring at us as we left, hidden in shadows, and they stood as still as statues as we drove off into the night.

I never saw their eyes.

# 18

We made it back to the station at around quarter past one and reported our findings to the chief, who reamed us on the spot for taking off like that. Once he was done, he told us to get some rest, because at first light the entire department was driving out to Kent to investigate and look for survivors.

Unfortunately, that never happened.

At around six in the morning, as we were waking up and heading to the station to prepare for the second trip in, it happened. A whopping seven-point-nine earthquake, the largest ever recorded for the state of Maine, was recorded at the spot where Kent stood. The aftershocks hit Bangor and caused intense structural damage, but fortunately no one was killed. Plenty had to go to the hospital for assorted injuries, but no one died from it, so that was alright.

By the time we reached Kent at around two in the afternoon, after taking care of our own people first, the town of Kent was gone. Completely. That damn crater was all that remained. It was still smoking.

Webster and I got out of the car and gaped at the hole where the town we had trudged through not half a day ago had stood. The crater was not bottomless, and we could see plenty of evidence of an earthquake at the bottom. What we didn't see was any evidence of a town; no building remains, no cars sticking out of the debris, not even a random piece of furniture or a lawn ornament. It was as if the earthquake had not only erased the town, but also erased any evidence of there ever being a town there at all.

Webster fell to his knees and began to cry, an utterly defeated man. I didn't try to cheer him up. I just stood by comforting him best I could, while looking down at our greatest failure.

# 19

There was an inquiry, of course. Both the state and federal governments wanted to know exactly what happened out there. This led to the forming of the infamous Kent Committee.

I'll spare you a lot of the gory details; most of that shit is in the public records, not that anyone ever goes looking for them. Our department and Orono were thoroughly investigated, and when I say they put us through the ringer, I mean they hung us from our balls and left us to dry. For six months, all that winter and into spring, we were bombarded with investigations, interrogations, and a full hearing in front of the committee. By the time it ended we got nothing for our troubles but a splitting headache and some of our best officers quitting and leaving for other ventures, too worn down to carry on.

Webster, Stugley, Trigger and I answered question after question regarding our handling of the case and everything we experienced, from that first phone call what felt like eons ago, the two failed attempts to get into Kent previously, the progression of events, our collaboration with Orono, and finally that last night. I told them everything I knew, except for two things: the Ichabod story, which was more for Webster to tell, and that last thing I saw leaving Kent. That would've just added more trouble.

There were times, I thought then and still think now, where it seemed like the committee was trying to find a scapegoat, someone to pin the blame on, and the five of us were just the easiest targets because of our involvement. They drilled me constantly over that last phone call with Amy Schumacher, made me relive it over and over. They said it was to keep the official record straight, but it felt more like they were trying to find any hole they could to pin on me. They never did, thankfully, but they sure tried.

Webster, I believe, got the worst of it, because at the end of the day it was his case. They pulled out his behavior, his rage, and his going against orders to go to Kent not once but twice, as if any of that mattered in the slightest. He fought back best he could, but a lot of that fire he had that week was gone. Kent broke him in a bad way that he never would get over. The fire was gone; a man twenty years older had taken his place.

I never knew what the final decree was – whether they took his badge or if he surrendered it willingly – but they got their scapegoat in the end. I was in the office with him as he cleared out his desk. It was just the two of us there; everyone else was out working or home for the night.

"This is so fucking unfair," I remember saying, the truest statement of the century.

"It's fine. I don't think I could keep working here anyway. Not after all that. Not after Jennings threw us under the bus."

Well, in the chief's defense, his only crime during that fiasco of an inquiry was brutal honesty. All he did was give an accurate and detailed account of everything; it's not like he knew the committee would use it all against us. Not that Webby would have listened to that then, but it's worth noting now.

He finished packing up his box and was rising to leave when I asked him the question that had been on my mind that whole time.

"Did you ever tell them? About Ichabod and your mother? Did you ask about a possible connection between Ichabod and Kent?"

He didn't answer right away. I wouldn't have blamed him if he never did, so it was a surprise to me when he finally did.

"Do me a favor, Jim?"

I nodded. He looked at me with that blank, haunted look that had permanently made its home on his face.

"Don't ever talk to me about Ichabod or Kent again," he said. "Ever. If you do, you and I are finished. Understand?"

I couldn't answer. I didn't know *how* to answer. I just gaped at him in silence that he took as answer enough. Without another word, he took his stuff and walked out of our station for the last time, leaving me all alone.

In the end, nothing else was ever done. The committee wrapped up their investigation and declared Kent lost. The crater where the town once stood was closed off and eventually filled in with fresh earth. The road that led there was turning into a jogging and bike path. All mentions of Kent were scrubbed from Maine's geography. Soon after the inquiry was done, Stugley and Trigger transferred to different divisions, and I never saw either of them again; what I heard of them after, I heard through others. Bangor moved on, and somehow, I moved on with them.

As they say, life turns on a dime.

# 20

The Bingo game had ended. A man who looked like Hans Moleman from the *Simpsons* had come out the winner; he held up his new rice cooker with pride, of course needing help from the staff to keep him steady in the process. Some of the old-timers were grumbling bitterly, but most of the others that had stayed this long were now shuffling off to bed. Better luck next week.

The girl's eyes were glistening. The old man was staring at one of the empty root beer bottles, tracing the mouth of it with his finger. They sat that way while most of the crowd puttered out, unaware as they had been all night of the tale that had been told there that night, the once-in-a-lifetime event that they knew nothing about.

Then the old man spoke again.

"Frank Mongeau died four months after our night trip to Kent," he said, and the girl physically started at the news. He smiled bitterly. "I know you were probably wondering why I didn't mention him during the inquiry. Well, that's why. He caught a cold from the trip that turned into double pneumonia. Add how weak his body had gotten from the arthritis that night, and he never stood a chance. He went peacefully, surrounded by family and friends, a tribute to his long, tireless career.

"Henry LaRose was killed in a car accident, this was in '66 or '67, one of those. Ran straight into a tree that sheered his car in half. Two-pound bags of cocaine were pulled from the wreckage. His mama, a thin woman with as much for brains as her late son, swore that it wasn't his, that he was taking it in as evidence, but funny thing about toxicology reports is, they don't lie. Trigger LaRose, who once shot a dime off a fence post from sixty yards, was so drugged up that he probably didn't even feel the tree that broke his body from head to toe."

"My God," the girl said weakly, and a tear slid down her cheek.

"I'll bet you're thinking that Derek Stugley died stopping a bank robbery, or maybe even during a prison riot or something. No such luck. It was a heart attack that did him in. No real surprise, of course. From what I heard, he was over three hundred pounds by the time his heart finally gave it up as a bad job. He had been in the front hallway of his apartment when he went down for the final count; the paramedics had to get in through the fire escape to get to him. That was in late December of '75, and I remember that because he was the last of our group that died...until I do, at least."

He had smirked bitterly when he related that, but now his face went somber again. The girl figured she knew why. There was one still unaccounted for, after all.

"Peter Webster...he had a tough time after Kent. He drifted around from one job to the other, never settling down in one position for very long. He lost contact with most of his old friends and became a loner. The drinking got worse around this time, too; he'd start the morning with a mimosa or two, a couple cocktails around noon, then down to Dell's at around four or five and just drink until closing. Someone would drive him home, and the cycle would begin again the next day. This went on for several years, as more and more people dropped out of his life, unable to bear witness to his spiral of self-destruction.

"He and I stayed close, though. I went through a rough patch of my own at that time, so he and I stuck to each other like two men drowning in the ocean...which, I suppose, is what we were. Most nights I was right down there at Dell's with him, drinking and laughing it up while we loaded up the jukebox with quarters, probably pissing off most of the other regulars.

"True to his request, I never mentioned Kent to him again. There were plenty of times where I felt we *should* have talked about it, tried to work through it together, help us to get over it. But I didn't. We were both trapped in a hole, and I was afraid that if he left me, I would be all alone, and in my mental state being alone was the worst thing that could happen to me. So, I kept my mouth shut. Might have been the worst decision of my life, but God as my witness I didn't mean any ill by it.

"As it turned out, I managed to crawl my way out of the hole myself; it was hard, but I did it. Webby, though...he never did. Oh, he tried, don't think he didn't. He went to the meetings, he spoke to the priests, he tried every program he could find. None of it worked. He was too lost in his grief, and I think deep down that maybe he didn't want to get out. They say those who feel guilty sometimes don't want to be saved, and I think that's what happened here. Either consciously or subconsciously, Web didn't want forgiveness. And he paid the price for it."

He sniffed, and the girl now saw tears forming in his own eyes. He reached for his water glass, forgetting it was empty. She offered her own, which had lay forgotten in the heat of the story, and he took a long gulp from it gratefully. He wiped his eyes with a napkin.

"Sorry...this part still hurts sometimes."

"We don't have to-"

"No, no, it's fine. We're almost done. Let's finish this up." He sat back in his chair. "One night, this was in '72 this was, Web went down to Dell's and ordered a round for everyone. He sat in the corner, listening to the Rolling Stones on the jukebox and eating peanuts, watching the others talk and laugh and drink. He himself only had water, or so I heard; I wasn't there that night. If I had been, maybe...well, no point continuing that thought.

"He paid for the next round as well, then went home and hanged himself from the kitchen fan. He was discovered three days later."

Her breath caught in her throat and came out in a gasp. He nodded.

"I read about it in the paper the day after he was found. I didn't cry then or at the funeral. Not that it didn't hurt – it felt like getting hit in the chest with a sledgehammer – but at the time it was just another dump of ice water on a long numb wound. Only four people attended his funeral. That's how much the world cared for the hero of Kent. Couldn't be bothered to attend his passing."

The silence that followed was deafening in its own awful way. The old man was remembering Webster as he was before Kent came into their lives, as the happy, hard-working man who would have done anything for anyone. Although that Webster had only been a part of his life for a very short time, he still remembered him fondly, and still rued the destruction of that man by forces no one could have predicted.

The girl wiped her eyes with her sleeve and let out a shaky breath.

"And you?" she asked him finally. "What happened to you?"

He smiled. "Me?"

# 21

I stayed with the Bangor police department for close to fifty years, eventually rising to the rank of detective sergeant. I was one of the lead investigators in the Effie MacDonald case in '65, and although we never did find out who killed her, my hard and careful work on that case caught the eye of a lot of notable big-wigs, and the recognition I got from them went a long way towards getting me past Kent. There were plenty of highs and plenty of lows, but I wouldn't have traded those five decades of work for anything in the world.

I had some hard times after Kent, as I said before. What ultimately snapped me out of it was waking up one morning after a hard night and stumbling to the bathroom like a zombie. I looked at myself in the mirror, with bloodshot, baggy eyes and a week's worth of stubble...and it was like I was looking into the eyes of a stranger. I didn't know who I was anymore. My path to sobriety began for the simple realization that I didn't want to live this way, that I didn't want Kent to rule over my life forever, like Webby.

It wasn't easy, coming back to the world. If anyone ever told you that sobriety was easy, they were a lying shit. I had the shakes and the worst headaches of my life, and I think I spent a week on the toilet puking my guts out. Eventually I got to the point where root beer could satisfy my cravings without killing me, and slowly I even managed to whittle that down to almost nothing. I think tonight's the most root beer I've had to drink since '68. I'm probably going to be pissing waterfalls tonight.

But it wasn't all bad either. I found a program that worked, and the people there were very supportive. My work, which had dipped during my time off the wagon, improved drastically as I dove into it to take my mind off my issues. I met my wife around that time, and she was a godsend to my life. Our marriage has outlived three major wars, four screaming children, and just about every world leader between 1965 and now, and if God can grace the two of us for just a few more years I imagine it'll continue to live strong. And in 1984, I won the Distinguished Service Medal for my long, prestigious career, one of the proudest days of my life.

After I retired around 2010 or so, we bought a house out here in Ogunquit; we spend most of our time here these days, when we're in state. My days since retirement have consisted of long walks, gardening, sailing, and travelling with my wife. We try to take a few trips a year all around the country, sometimes to different parts of Europe. Obviously, the last year or so we couldn't, but we're planning one major Europe trip for next summer. Our final send-off, if you will.

But no matter what is going on, either in the world or in my life, I make it a point to be in Bangor every November. Mostly to spend Thanksgiving with family and any old friends who are still alive...but also to pay respects.

Kent left its mark on all of us who lived through it. I was just the lucky one who pushed past it and moved on. I couldn't tell you why I was the one to have the stronger will to survive any more than I could tell you why God invented the platypus, but I did. And it's because I did and the others didn't that I have a duty to carry their memory with me, as well as the scars we received that night. Living has been a wonderful thing, but it certainly came with a cost.

In 2010, on the fiftieth anniversary of the Kent disaster, I was standing at Peter Webster's grave, as I always ended that week with. I had placed my flowers and had run out of things to talk about. I stared down at the grave, at his name and the dates carved into it, and something came over me.

I thought of Webster, one of the best friends I ever had, who had only tried to do the right thing. I thought of Frank and Trigger and Stugley, who were just doing their jobs. I thought of Ernest Lanslow, and the secrets he had taken with him. I thought of Amy Schumacher and the people of Kent, who had done nothing wrong to anyone and yet had been taken away all the same.

Mostly I thought about how young we all were, how we had the world at our fingertips, and how one awful week took all that away from us.

I stood staring at my best friend's grave, thinking all those things...and something happened. Something I had never done before, but something long, long overdue.

I fell to my knees and cried fifty years' worth of tears.

# Epilogue

It was closing time now. The Bingo game had cleared out, and the staff was now wiping down the tables with that ready-to-go-home fervor. The jukebox had shut down for the night, and the silence that came with it seemed fitting; what else was there to say? The only two patrons still not making much of a hurry to leave were the old man and the girl.

He placed the empty water glass down.

"And that, missy," he said, "is just about everything. The whole story of Kent, told in a couple of hours. And just in time, too, by the looks of it."

The girl sat there, tears streaking down her face openly now. It was the same reaction he remembered his wife having when he told her, all those years ago.

"And you never..." she began, shaking her head. "And you never found any reason for it? Nothing?"

He shook his head. "Never a thing. I tried, you know. Looked for years. Eventually I gave up. After a time, the why just...stopped being important."

"How?"

"Because I realized over time that why is an inconsequential question. Why did Roanoke happen? Or the Malaysian flight? Why did Dennis Martin go missing in front of his family? Why did the *Mary Celeste* show up without its crew? Even the well-known things, like JFK getting shot. Sometimes bad things, even the most fucked up things imaginable, just happen. They don't need a why. They just *are*."

He let that statement hang in the air for a moment. It was a lame summarization to this whole tale, but he couldn't think of a better way to phrase it.

She still sat there, wrapping her head around it. He smiled gently.

"It's past my bedtime, little lady. I've told all I know."

She nodded, wiping her eyes. She wanted to thank him, apologize for the trouble, and thank him for indulging her curiosity, but somehow doing so felt woefully inadequate given all she had heard.

"I won't lie to you, miss. Telling this story has been painful for me. Tonight has ripped open a lot of old wounds and opened doors that have long been closed. Add that I'm probably going to be at the toilet for the rest of the night and I don't think I'm going to be getting a good night's sleep for a while."

"I'm sorry, I didn't mean to-" she began, but he interrupted her.

"And yet, when I think back on that time and how we all were, I can't help but feel a wave of nostalgia wash over me. I do believe there is some good in remembering, if only that it preserves youth in the past. And it's nice to find someone who was genuinely interested to hear about it. I mean my wife was, but you know...obligation."

They laughed at that, not bitterly, not to get over tragedy, but a good hearty laugh. It brightened up his face, and in the moment the girl could see the young man he had been on the day when one phone call had changed his life forever.

"So, I thank you, miss...I'm sorry, I don't believe I ever got your name."

"Oh, Allie." She smiled. "Allie Lewis."

"Well, Miss Allie Lewis, I thank you for spending a couple of hours listening to this old man relive the past."

"It was my pleasure, sir." She stood up, slinging her bag back over her shoulder. "I can't thank you enough for telling me what really happened. I'm never going to forget this."

"I sure hope not." And then his face hardened again, and she felt herself tensing up, bracing for what was next. "And now, in return, I will give you one last piece of advice to take with you wherever you go next."

She nodded wearily. He had been talking for over two hours now, and his voice was probably forever scarred into her brain along with his tale, but she still listened carefully.

He leaned forward again, his eyes never leaving hers, and hers never leaving his.

"If you are ever in Bangor, Maine, you may see a road leading to the west. You may feel compelled to follow it. If you follow it about twenty miles, you'll find a large daisy field. Daisies are just about the only thing that grows there anymore. A town used to stand there. You may be compelled to stay there a while and look around. See if you can find any clues to where the town went. Don't do that. Instead, turn around and go back. Better yet, just walk by the path altogether and move on."

"Okay..."

"I'm serious." The look in his eyes was now maddening, and she shrank back from it. "Don't go looking for Kent. Trust me, there's nothing for you out there. Nothing."

The girl nodded sharply, but there was something in her eyes that the old man didn't quite trust. Without another word, she smiled in farewell, then turned and walked back out of his life the same way she had come in.

The old man watched her go, wondering for the first time if maybe telling her had been a mistake. He wondered if he had done nothing but fuel her desire to look for the truth further. But it wasn't his place to judge her. She would either heed his warning or she wouldn't. She would find out whatever she needed to for herself.

He paid his bill, thankful that she had kept her drink of choice free to not add to the expenses, then grabbed his coat and went home. His wife would be asleep when he got in. That was alright.

That was perfectly okay.

# Don't miss out!

Visit the website below and you can sign up to receive emails whenever Thomas Horan publishes a new book. There's no charge and no obligation.

https://books2read.com/r/B-A-MHVT-SYVYB

**BOOKS 2 READ**

Connecting independent readers to independent writers.

# Also by Thomas Horan

Kent

Watch for more at https://sickslickproductions.com/.

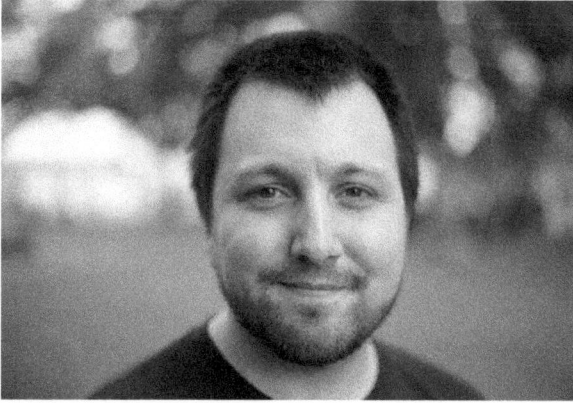

# About the Author

Thomas Horan is a middle school English teacher, Youtuber, and author. His next book, The Dark Man, is currently seeking agent representation and will be published in the near future. He is an avid movie watcher and gamer, and enjoys reading (primarily Stephen King) and going for walks to clear his mind.

He currently resides in Gardner, Massachusetts with his fiancé Sasha and stepson Nelson.

Read more at https://sickslickproductions.com/.

# About the Publisher

9 798201 190477